Gone Are The Days!

Gone Are The Days!

Gaurav Sharma

KALPAZ

ISBN: 978-93-5128-237-2

Price: ₹ 190/-

First Published, 2016

Published by

Kalpaz Publications
C-30, Satyawati Nagar,
Delhi – 110052
E-mail: kalpaz@hotmail.com
Ph.: 9212142040

Printed at: G. Print Process, Delhi

Cataloging in Publication Data—DK
Courtesy: D.K. Agencies (P) Ltd. <docinfo@dkagencies.com>

Sharma, Gaurav, 1992- author.
Gone are the days! / Gaurav Sharma.
pages cm
Novel.
ISBN 9789351282372

1. Sharma, Gaurav, 1992- —Childhood and youth—Fiction.
2. Indic fiction (English) I. Title.

PR9499.4.S53G66 2016 DDC 823.92 23

Contents

Acknowledgements 9

Author's Note & Disclaimer 11

1. A Sudden Reminder 13
2. Even Before I was Born 23
3. Initial Days 29
4. My First School 35
5. Life at N.S.D.A.V. 39
6. See You! Mommy 45
7. Last Year in Sitamarhi 51
8. Goodbye, Home! 61
9. Enroute Chandigarh 67
10. The City Beautiful 73
11. Am I Really in Delhi? 77
12. Welcome to Life! 83
13. The Concept of Jugaad 87
14. Guess What? 91
15. Get Me Out of Here! 95

16. The Chits of My Fate 101
17. Doomsday 105
18. What Next? 109
19. A High School Without Uniform 115
20. Life in ~~JISM~~ JIMS! 121
21. Friends for Life, As They Say 127
22. Reality Check 141
23. Farewell Till We Meet Again 145
24. Welcome to Canada 'Mr. Sharma!' 151
25. A College Where India and China Co-exist, Peacefully! 155
26. My 'Canadian' Friends 159
27. Delhi Calling 165
28. I Am a Victorian! 169
29. The Crux 173

Dedication

I dedicate this book to all my readers, irrespective of whether they purchased my book, illegally obtained a copy, downloaded it or borrowed it from someone else. Some went ahead and directly asked me to send them a softcopy of my book. Special salute to them as well.

ACKNOWLEDGEMENTS

Time for some formalities! Just kidding.

A big thanks to my publishers who took the pain of going through my mess and made necessary arrangements so that you all can read this book. Negotiating and deciding on royalty percentage was a bit challenging, though. Never mind! Money generation was never a motive behind writing.

My love to all those who keep me close to their hearts without any terms and conditions attached to it. Mentioning their names here is not that vital. What holds importance is being grateful to them, which I am and forever will be. Now that you are reading this statement, five months after it was written, the list of people who keep me close to their hearts has become shorter.

That would be all. Nobody else helped me write this book.

Author's Note & Disclaimer

Fiction means something which is fabricated as opposed to facts. Fiction bears no relation of any type, or in any form with reality. And my novel is just that, a work of fiction. I want to make it absolutely clear to my esteemed readers that names, characters, businesses, places, events and incidents depicted in this novel are either the products of my imagination or used in a fictitious manner. Any resemblance to actual persons, living or dead, or actual events is purely coincidental. I have tried to recreate events, locales, and conversations from my own memories of them. In order to maintain their anonymity in some instances, I have changed the names of individuals and places.

In order to express my emotions based on the intensity of plot, I have used such language which might surpass the standards of syntaxical decency and hence, may be categorised as 'profane' and/or 'vulgar'. However, I expect from my readers to show an adequate amount of discretion and maturity. Nonetheless, if you are among those 'decent innocent souls' on earth and have any problem or feel uncomfortable with such language, I caution you not to proceed further. To get your money back, contact me. You shall find me on the web, or log on to www.authorgauravsharma.com; Gotcha?

Oh! C'mon, be a sport *pancho!*

—**Gaurav Sharma**

July 20, 2016
Victoria, Canada

1

A Sudden Reminder

It was a quiet afternoon of July 2014. Sun was burning to its fullest as summers in Delhi are hot as hell. It often reaches up to 45 degrees Celsius and sometimes even higher than that. But I did not give a shit for I was sipping chilled chocolate shake while playing with my newly bought Nintendo Wii; and above all, I had my ass in the comfort of an air conditioned room.

After few minutes I heard a distant sound which was gradually coming nearer. 'Dug dug dug dug....' this was now banging in my head and I realised I knew that sound. It was an idiot with a Royal Enfield Thunderbird 500.

'Hey, buddy! Don't you think you are late?' Asked Ranbijay even before entering my room. Ranbijay, the idiot I mentioned above is my friend from college time.

'Late?? For what!! Do we have a date...hahaha'.

'Oh come on! I can't believe you really forgot'. And he raised one of his eyebrows.

There was an awkward silence...The silence before catastrophe.

'Oh Shit! Shit!! Shit!!! It's already 2:30!! Where have you been...you jerk! You were supposed to take me there!'

'Okay calm down. Now that I am here, everything will be sorted'. He flaunted while showing the keys of his brand new motorbike. I switched off my game and we both rushed out.

'No, wait!' I shouted. 'Now what??' asked Ranbijay…I ran back and grabbed my glass of chocolate shake.

'You will remain YOU Gaurav.'

'And what do you mean by YOU here?'

'I mean you will remain an idiot Gaurav…hahaha'.

'Shut up and rush, you fool'.

That day I had my IELTS speaking test at 3:30 PM and Ranbijay was supposed to take me there on his bike. But somehow it slipped completely out of my mind…well maybe because of my new video game. Luckily, he didn't forget.

'So why didn't you call me yester-night'? I asked loudly as it was difficult to speak or hear while on that motorbike.

'Why was I supposed to call you?'

'To remind me.'

'Remind you?? About what??'

'Argghhh….about today; about my test.'

'Well…am I your reminder? I planned to take you by surprise on that.'

'Surprise!! My foot! You scared the hell out of me. It…it was a minor heart attack dude, and you call it a surprise!! Bullshit.'

'Okay don't lose your calm now. I am taking you there. Relax; buddy.'

'Hey! Watch out…speed breaker!' I shouted.

'Hold tight!' said Ranbijay and he accelerated instead of slowing down.

'Hey slow down dude.'

'Slow?? It's not in my dictionary.'

'Oye oye…it's a motor-bike, not a plane. Just slow down; are you crazy!!'

'Life is going to be a bumpy ride ahead buddy, sit tight and fasten your seatbelt….yoohoo..'

'Seat…what? Oh hell! I am never going to take another ride with you, dickhead. This is the very first and last time, you jerk!' I shouted in a frightened voice.

'Okay…by the way I thought you will be returning to home with me only. But it's cool if you take a bus and…'

'Well…probably it's the first and second last time I am riding with you….haha.'

'So where now? Left or right??'

'I don't know the route!! Let me turn on this goddamn navigation for you.' I shouted.

'Gaurav, is there anything on earth you know about?!'

'Yeah! That you are an idiot and will always remain an idiot.'

'I guess its left turn'. Said Ranbijay and he took that turn. By the way, Google Maps was still loading on my phone.

'Well…you are very good at this, I must say.'

'Will you clarify AT WHAT?'

'At GUESS work!!' haha…I said to pull his leg.

'Okay cool…so guess what!'

'What?'

'I am taking a U-turn now! Do hell with your test, Gaurav. I am done now!!'

'Woo…HAHA…I was just kidding dude. I swear you are not even good at guess work!! In fact, you are good for nothing, believe me!!'

'Bwahahaha…' and we both laughed like anything. Some passers-by stared at us as if laughing while driving on the road is a crime in the country.

'But dude, I am not talking to you now. This is not how you treat your friends…I mean, every time we meet, you start cracking jokes on me, Gaurav. Man! I am not supposed to be harassed like this! Its verbal violence in its purest form…This is simply not done!' He said with a very helpless frustrated voice and was expecting some shitty apologies from my side.

'So you sure you wouldn't talk to me anymore?' I pretended to be assertive.

'Hell yeah, man!! I've got so many other friends who treat me with respect that I deserve.'

'Respect you deserve…bwahaha?!! Okay! By the way, I was thinking of taking you out for dinner tonight! But now that we are not talking to each other anymore and I don't respect you enough, there is no point of having dinner together.'

'No! I mean it's not that bad you know…I like when you crack jokes on me. You are really a great friend to have, Gaurav.'

'What did you just say? You bastard…!'

'Yes. I am Serious. You are a great friend. My brother from another mother.'

'Haha…' we both laughed again.

You know, offering delicious food to Ranbijay will make him do anything for you. Give him a good meal and he can even die for you. Such a foodie he is.

'Here comes your test centre.' Ranbijay stopped and I got off his bike. He parked his bike and came where I was standing.

'You see such an awesome biker I am, it's not even three.' He showed his wrist watch to me. I could barely see the dial through cracked glass of his watch, it was 2:58 PM.

'Oh, whatever! By the way, it will take around half an hour or so for me to get done with the test and other formalities. What will you do in the meantime?'

'What?! Am I not supposed to come with you?'

'Nope. They wouldn't allow you to enter the centre. You will have to wait in waiting area only.'

'Holy shit!! I did not come all the way along with you to wait here in this goddamn waiting area! I drove you here in fucking 50 degrees Celsius! You have to do something; I am just not going to sit here!

'Excuse me pal! This is IELTS; you understand? This is International English Language Testing System...not a Bihar Board exam where candidates are accompanied by their friends, neighbours and relatives until they finish writing the test... ha ha ha!! Relax buddy, it's just a matter of time.'

'Exactly! It's a matter of a whole damn half an hour buddy. What will I do till then?' He asked in helplessness.

'Do whatever you want to do. What's your favourite pass time?' I asked in a suggestive tone.

'Well...this area does not even have hot chicks roaming around...I would have checked out some.'

'Aargh! Want to play Iron Man 3 official game?' I asked.

'Oh shut up! As if Tony Stark gave you the original premium version of game?' He said in a disappointed tone.

'You don't believe me fucker!? Okay here you go…' I took out my smart phone and showed him the original Iron Man 3 official game.

'Are you kidding me!? I don't believe this shit…don't tell me you actually bought this game for five thousand rupees!! If I were you, I would have spent that money on customising my bike or clubbing or something else!'

'Yes my dear…you are not the only one on this planet who loves action games and that too like Iron Man. And luckily, I am not you. I would not spend a single penny on a heavy piece of metallic shit that makes too much noise.'

'Give me that and go! And no need to hurry up now, take your time I am waiting here only…Ha ha!' he grabbed my phone quickly in excitement.

'You mean, rascal'…I muttered. I could see his eyes holding tremendous allure in them for my phone and that game.

I left him there in the waiting area and entered the main facility. It was simply humongous and seemed like a sub-city. People were roaming here and there. As the test centre was built inside a shopping complex, it had a mixed crowd all over. I searched for my centre in the site map of the complex and it indicated that I had to go to the seventh floor. I could not easily figure out the way to reach my centre and hence concluded that that fucking complex was real 'complex'. I looked for the elevators but could not figure out their location as I was about to be late for the test. I was in a hurry. I noticed that escalators too were out of service. 'What the hell?!' I grumbled as soon as I realised I had to take the stairs and climb up to the seventh floor. You realise? SEVENTH fucking floor!!

I began climbing. Soon after reaching the third floor I was out of breath. I had no other option but to keep going as fast as

I could. I somehow made up to the fourth floor. 'OH FUCK!'...It just came from within; I don't know why. I kept on climbing like a turtle. By the time I reached the sixth floor I was almost dead. I began swearing at myself, escalators, elevators, IELTS itself and whoever the fuck built that shopping complex. Finally, I reached the seventh floor and saw my test centre. 'Holy Mary mother of Jesus!' I murmured in relief. It was a restaurant-bar type of place. I was pretty excited and nervous at the same time.

I went inside; a fat lady checked my passport and pushed me into the scanning machine. Holy shit! That scanner was actually showing everything inside my clothes. It felt as if I was naked. Believe me, it's not fun to watch yourself naked in front of strangers. Anyways, I passed the security check and entered. What I saw inside was not-at-all different from a torture room. Candidates with pale faces and helpless looks, just like goats in a goddamn slaughter house! I mean, it's just a test for God's sake...an English speaking test, right? I sat on a chair and waited for my turn. After a while, I heard my name and candidate number. It was my turn now. Through all my way to the test room even I was feeling like a scared sheep, I admit. Well...it happens sometimes!

'May I come in?' I asked with a choked throat.

'Oh yes! Come in please.'

She was a beautiful lady with very confident voice. I don't know if she was younger or elder than me. Who the hell cares about age anyway; the only thing that matters, is beauty!

'Have a seat.' She said.

'Thank you!' it's too hot out there. I muttered.

'Do you want some water...? Shall we begin the test?'

Well…I was about to say 'yes! I need some water. Can't you see I am sweating like a sinner in church?'; but her second question just killed all my thirst and I said, 'No. I am good to go.'

Just because she was confident enough to influence me upon taking the test ASAP, I changed my answer…I changed my mind and decided not to drink water even though I was very thirsty. It might be a simple and ordinary instance for others but not for me. In that very moment, I discovered the relationship between confidence and influence. I am an active learner, you see!

'Mr. Sharma from now onwards, all our conversation will be recorded as per the regulations of IELTS. Are you okay with that?'

'Is it going to change anything if I am not okay with this recording part?' I asked with a fake smile hoping for some positive response. I was trying to act smart and cool in front of her. Though I needed 6.5 bands overall in the test, which was peanuts for me, I knew; Yet I had to impress her; I needed maximum bands for the test as I had to show-off my bands among friends and family. After all I had paid Ten thousand rupees for that test. We middle class people…you know!

'Yes! It will make a remarkable change Mr. Sharma. You will be disqualified if the test is not recorded.' She replied sarcastically even with a better fake smile. Quite a positive response from her side. Huh?

'Then I have no other choice but to take the test while recording is on.' I said helplessly.

'Why would you ask such a stupid question, lady?' I was thinking in my mind and then…

'Procedure, Mr. Sharma; I had to officially inform you about this voice recording thing.'

'Oh! Shit. How did she get to know what's going inside my mind?' I wondered.

The test began finally. She introduced herself briefly. I got to know that her name was Ashley Judy. After introducing herself she asked me for my introduction. I spoke about myself, my (not so impressive) academic qualifications, boring hobbies and some other random stuff. And I thought I nailed it! But good luck and I are enemies for life. We just don't go hand in hand!

'Tell me something about your life, Mr. Sharma. Things you remember from the past, your childhood, good and bad experiences and everything. Be as descriptive as possible.' She asked in a very firm tone.

'What! I mean, seriously!? Don't you really have anything else to ask, lady? What kind of a question is it?' I thought in a very shocked and surprised state of mind as she asked something out of expectation. That moment made me realise that Ashley Judy was very moody and she burnt all my preparation into ashes.

'Do you want me to start from the very beginning?'

'Yes. Start from the beginning of time.'

'I don't mean to skip this question, but it's a very long and boring story, you see?'

'Don't you worry Mr. Sharma, as far as the boring part is concerned I am sure you will have something which is at least not as boring as people ranting and chanting self-prepared answers to show off their 'limited' command over English language. You are my last candidate for the day and I have ample time left with me. So just go ahead. Give me something worth listening.'

It was quite a task for me. I was pretty nervous thinking about what I was going to say and most importantly, I was worried about my cell phone which was in the hands of that nutcase, Ranbijay. I knew he was just going to molest my phone electronically by pushing it to its technical limits. Last time when I got my phone back from him, I had tens of pornographic web pages opened in its browser. I did not want him to install some shitty applications in my phone this time.

About an hour ago I was living the moment, enjoying my life and suddenly I found myself trapped in that hell. Everything was just a hodgepodge at that very moment. But I had no other choice but to face that 'situation critical'. I took a deep breath, closed my eyes and in a fraction of a second, I was in a different world. It felt as if I was seeing my past life and what all took place even before my birth with a different point of view. My brain gathered all information and processed that data into a film. It started flashing at the back of my mind and I began by saying...

'Ma'am, you got me. Here you go!'

2

EVEN BEFORE I WAS BORN

Not so very long ago in time, there lived a wise businessman Gandharv in a small town of Sitamarhi which lies in the state of Bihar and shares its vicinity with Nepal. Sitamarhi is a remarkable place in Hindu mythology. Its history goes back to Treta Yuga when Sita, a Hindu goddess and the wife of Lord Rama sprang to life out of an earthen pot when Raja Janak was ploughing the field somewhere near Sitamarhi to impress upon Lord Indra for rain.

Gandharv and his wife Kamla had five children; two sons and three daughters. They all resided in a big house built on the bank of river Lakhandei which passes through a channel in the main town. His house was more of a mansion. It was equipped with the then modern amenities and surrounded by a lush green environment having a beautiful garden at the back. That garden had guava trees, mango trees, maze, sugarcane, tomato, peas, litchi, berries and many other fruits and vegetables planted. Each and every day before going to his shop, Gandharv would work in his garden, cut the grasses, plant new vegetables, supply water and do everything required to maintain its beauty.

This one was a typical religious Brahmin family where each and every member was equally important. Their main principle of leading a peaceful life was 'eat, live, work and pray'. Gandharv believed in Lord Shiva. Each day he would bare foot go to a nearby temple and offer water upon Shiva-lingam. Once every month he would clean temple idols and premises. Though this family lived in the state of Bihar, yet its roots were in Punjab. Gandharv had established a small business of motor parts in Sitamarhi. At that time his shop, 'Shankar Motors (India)' was the only one in town which catered automobile industry. Every day Gandharv would leave his home after having a light breakfast at seven in the morning. After reaching the shop on his 'Hero' bicycle he would clean the floor with a broom. He had taken a subscription of Hindi national newspaper 'Hindustan'. That newspaper was always found under the counter of the shop as a delivery man would flick it from the space left between the floor and closed shutter. He would thoroughly read the paper on a regular basis.

Eldest daughter Sangita would parcel his lunch prepared by Kamla. Upon handing over the tiffin box to her father, Sangita would receive five rupees from him. She always shared that money equally among all her siblings. Each one would get a rupee and often spend that amount in the evening. Every night around nine Gandharv would return to home. All of the children would sit in the chairs and open their books to impress their father. They often held their books upside down in excitement and nervousness! Time passed by and those children were not kiddos anymore.

Gandharv's elder son Pankaj was a young boy with a vibrant personality. He had many good friends who always stood by him no matter what. Pankaj was a fitness freak. Every morning he would wake up at five and complete one round of the entire town while jogging. Pankaj used to sing very well. He also had a remarkable inclination towards ghazals and folk songs. His passion for music was so immense that he had the largest collection of audio cassettes of various ghazal maestros like

Ghulam Ali, Jagjit Singh, Ahmed Hussain and many more singing personalities.

Soon after completing studies he decided to help his father with the family business. He learnt each and every aspect of the business art and worked with full dedication so as to expand his business as much as possible. Soon that business grew and expanded at a pace that everyone got to know about Gandharv and his shop. His so called small business was reaching new heights. Mechanics, drivers, engineers and all those related to motor industry started recognising Gandharv, his family and the shop.

In a small town like Sitamarhi, it's very hard to remain hidden as any news or happening spreads like a jungle fire within no time. Gandharv became the king of automobile spare parts in his town. His simplicity, honesty and hard work made him a respectable man in the society. People would enjoy his company and seek his advice before doing any important work.

Eventually, Gandharv got all his children married in great families with huge pomp and show. Pankaj got married to Puja, a simple girl from a very rich family based in Delhi. Puja's father, Mr. Ved Prakash was a renowned multi-millionaire businessman and philanthropist. He too had a big house which was more of a castle, luxury cars that were no less than palaces on wheels, the state-of-the-art infrastructure with marvelous looks, over hundreds of servants, workers, cooks and what not! Such was the kingdom of Mr. Ved Prakash and Puja was the princess of that kingdom.

Initially, it was a bit difficult for her to adjust in a completely different place with different people, society and customs. Someone who used to travel in cars was now relying on rickshaws and someone who always saw the outside world glittering would spend hours and more hours in darkness as the then condition of electricity in Bihar was horrible. More or less same as Narendra Modi, once gone from home nobody knows when it will return and for how many hours. All the more, Puja had never seen mosquitoes, flies, lizards and bugs in her life before marriage. But she adapted very well and devoted everything to her new family in Sitamarhi. After all, it's family that matters and not rickshaws, electricity or mosquitoes...if you know what I mean.

A lot was changed in Gandharv's family after this marriage. He used to leave for the shop by 9 AM as it was Pankaj's duty to open the shop at 7 AM and do the cleaning. He got more time to look after his beautiful garden. He would send Pankaj back to home after reaching the shop. His lunch would now parcel by Pankaj instead of Sangita and prepared by Puja with some assistance and guidance from her mother-in-law, Kamla. Also, Gandharv would return back to home at around 7 PM and let Pankaj close the shop at 11 in the night. Everything was going good and a year had passed.

Now it was time for Puja to visit her parents for the first time after marriage. Also, she was about to give birth to a child. She discussed the matter with elders and suggested the dates for reservations.Those were the times when train ticket booking was a hell of a mission (impossible) in small towns. There were only two counters at Sitamarhi railway station which could get reservations done. Never ending lines, dirty walls, bad odour, a lot of frustration and 'full body bone-cracking massage' were some of the complimentary features that used to come with ticket booking. There were no travel agents in small towns and IRCTC and online websites were something unheard and unimagined. Luckily, one of Pankaj's school friend's father was the then Station Master of Sitamarhi and he got all things sorted.

After 15 days Puja and Pankaj departed for Delhi. Their journey was supposed to take about 17 hours. Everything changes for betterment with time as change is constant, but exceptions are always there. The legacy of railways is one of those exceptions, for their train was running eight hours behind the scheduled time. Well…some things never change. After about 25 hours of the tiring journey, they reached Delhi. Puja had travelled by train for the second time in her life (first time when she came to Sitamarhi) and her experience from both journeys was memorable. Memorably devastating, to be specific. All thanks to Indian Railways!

Pankaj came back to Sitamarhi to look after his business. It dates back to March 4, 1992; the day was Wednesday and clock ticked 3 AM sharp. It was a dark, chilly and silent night with no stars in the sky. The moon was glowing like a lantern with dim flame. Puja called her mother in a painful voice. Very soon she was taken to a hospital nearby. After an hour or so there was a wave of contentment throughout maternity ward as Puja and Pankaj had their first child. Yes, I had come to join the party at 4:20 AM. The time of my birth is one of those baseless reasons why people guess I am (over) smart "420" (Section 420 of Indian Penal Code deals with deception and cheating).

Anyway, since mommy was at maternal grandpa's place in Delhi and papa was in Sitamarhi, a telegram was sent from Delhi to inform papa and grandpa about my birth. Families from both the sides were celebrating. Religious ceremonies were performed as it is performed in almost every Hindu family so as to give a name to the newly born. After performing some serious astrological shit, the priest suggested that the name should start from letter G. Grandma and papa suggested 'Gautam' whereas mommy and grandpa suggested 'Gaurav'. Then few phone calls were made to all my Bua (sisters of my father), Mama (brother of my mother), Uncle, neighbour(s) asking for suggesting a fancy name which starts with letter G. Some elders said 'Ganesh' others suggested 'Gopal', 'Garv', 'Girish' and what not! Today I often think that, had my neighbours been as jerk as some of the fellow students I met in my college, JIMS, they would have suggested a name which starts with G and rhymes with 'Pandu'. Most people must've got it, for everybody else's knowledge it's just an abusive slang. Luckily that was not the case and everybody agreed on one name, 'Gaurav' which means "Honour" / "Pride". From there I got my name.

Though my name does not resemble with my attitude as I always had a hard time doing anything to make my family or friends feel proud of me, yet I am satisfied with it as I have not done anything that made my family or friends ashamed of me. So, for me, not doing anything dishonouring is also subject to pride and honour. I keep it simple.

3

Initial Days

About a month after my birth mommy returned to Sitamarhi with me. Papa, grandpa, and grandma were there to receive us at the station. They saw me for the first time! It seemed that they were the happiest people on earth. I wonder at times, life would have blazed to glory if e-mail, WhatsApp and internet were there almost 24 years back. Today, we just don't realise the significance of technology and resources. It seems to us as if these assets were already there from the beginning of time but sadly, they were not. Anyway, it was worth the wait for papa, grandpa and grandma. Soon after I arrived in the neighbourhood, people gathered in my house to take the first look of newly born i.e. me.

As mommy often describes to me, they were squeezing my cheeks and kissing on my forehead. Some extra-emotional women used to give me a hefty thwack! I don't know how I survived that. Another year had gone in a blink of an eye. By that time, I had started murmuring and recognising things like table, fan, ear, eyes, nose and some other useless stuff. By the time I turned two years old, grandma appointed two maids to assist mommy with household works. Those were more of neighbours than just maids. Both were sisters and Guddi and Munni were their names. I grew up with them…well, initially!

Apart from assisting mommy in her kitchen works, Guddi and Munni used to play a lot of 'self-experimented' games with me just to see me laughing.

Things were changing remarkably. Grandpa would take me to the temple with him. Huge bells, beautiful idols and long-bearded priests were subject to fascination for me. Then there was this statue of 'Nandi' ox situated in front of Shiva temple that would scare the hell out of me. Despite the terror of that statue in my mind, one thing that kept me interested in visiting temple daily with grandpa was the 'Prasad' (eatable offerings made to the God, but at the end, we eat it all because God does not give a shit!). It used to be simply tasty and sweet. After all, I used to think with my taste buds and not brains. So I kept on going to the temple with grandpa.

Papa would take me to the shop and make me sit on the counter. Every known customer who would come to the shop asked papa about me. Some overwhelmed chaps would take me with them to their garages and factories just to play and have fun with me. A small kid is no less than a toy for some people and I was their stress buster of all time. I would go neat and clean and come back to shop dipped with grease, oil, and lubricants. Business was in my blood and I was doing well at it. I was attracting more and more people to my shop. Though they all were not there to buy something yet they were there in the shop. Soon I remembered some names and prices of the goods in my shop. Papa and grandpa would laugh after hearing the names of those products from me. After all, they had a valid reason as I would call "deck lid" as dick-lid.

Time flew and I became three years old. Now I would question everything according to my own understandings of things going around me. I had developed an advanced sense of recognition. Also, I had a competent command over the language by that time. I could understand what others used to say and frame my own stupid sentences and phrases.

Of all the things I used to question about, what grandpa does in the garden was most concerning for me. Every morning I would see him going to the garden with a machete-cum-reaper in his hand. Initially, it would scare me. I often ask him to take me to the garden with him but grandma would not allow me. She was afraid of me going out into the garden as I could be bitten by bugs, worms, insects or anything like that. Grandmothers are always too concerned about their grandchildren. Grandma would name all the creatures with a scary look on her face. She used to think that naming those creatures with emphasis would stop me from going in there by creating fear inside my mind. Well, she was wrong as her way of stopping me added fuel to the fire and made me even more curious to see the garden and its creatures. As a result, I decided to go to the garden at any cost.

Cry and tears are kids' best weapons for making others do whatever kids want them to do. Without delaying a minute, I too started crying and softly banging my head against the wall. It was one of my favourite tricks to get things done swiftly. After few minutes of drama, grandma agreed and sent me with grandpa. That was probably the first time I saw my garden after becoming consciously active. What I saw in there was no less than a wonderland for me. Beautiful trees and plants packed with colourful fruits and vegetables. The green grass seemed to be a fine carpet gifted by nature to us. Most importantly, I discovered what grandpa used to do in the garden with that machete-like reaper. He would cut unwanted grass and branches, collect and dispose dry leaves and do everything else required to maintain the beauty and fruitfulness of the garden.

Few days had gone with me visiting garden daily along with grandpa. I requested him to allow me to work in the garden just like he used to do. He could not resist anymore and granted the permission with a broad smile on his face. It felt as if I won a battle. To gain unrestricted access to the garden was a hell of an achievement for me. Grandpa bought me a plastic machete-like reaper, somewhat similar in looks to his reaper. We would work like a team.

Every morning grandpa and I would wake up around seven and raid the garden. He would do what he had been doing ever since that garden came into existence and I would play with the soil, leaves and of course my plastic reaper! I came across many creatures grandma used to tell me about. They were snails, earthworms, insects, bugs and birds. My close contact with these creatures on a daily basis would make me more and more fearless each day. Because of grandpa, I came closer to nature and realised its significance.

Mommy began my home schooling since I turned out two. By the time I was three years old I could count numbers till 40, recite ABCD…and do some other random stuff. A for apple, B for ball, C for cat and D for dog was completely settled in my mind. I used to correct grandma upon saying A for aeroplane and B for bat because it was not right! At that time, A was for apple and B had nothing to do with the bat but the ball. Kids are innocent at such an age. But now I realise the long-term impact of mugging up things in our education system. It all starts at an early age. That fine line between information and knowledge is fading away day-by-day. Who gives a shit by the way!

Since I was an active learner and used to grasp things very easily, papa thought it was time to put me into formal schooling. It was time for me to enter play school.

At that time Sitamarhi had only three famous schools. These were St. Joseph Mission School, N.S.D.A.V. Public School and

Saraswati Vidya Mandir. Play schools like Kidzee, Mother's Pride, Eurokids and Shemrock were next-century dreams. Grandpa and papa started researching for the best school for me. They got to know that only St. Joseph had a 'Baby Class' dedicated to tiny tots before they begin their studies officially. Without any doubt, they decided to put me in that school. I still remember grandma taking me to a shop nearby and asking me to pick any school bag of my choice. I pointed toward a black and silver one. After that, she bought me a nice small water bottle with a long strap attached to it. I was totally unaware of the situation and took that day as a shopping fiesta. Things became more joyous when papa bought a cartoon lunch box one night. I kept asking him what is that all about but he smiled every time and said I was going to play with other kids soon. Well…I had no idea how soon.

4

My First School

One fine morning of April 1995 papa took me to my very first school for the very first time. I was pretty excited to presume that school days were going to be fun days. Because it was not important for me to take a bath and go for pooping every morning, I got ready in less than 10 minutes. Mommy packed my bag with lots of toffees for my future friends. She also put inside my bag that fancy cartoon lunch box which papa had bought the other day. I carried my small school bag and hung my water bottle around the neck. I rapidly climbed upon papa's bicycle and we flew toward our destination. It was just a bicycle; but when papa used to ride that, it would become a supersonic plane gliding on road and I would often make awkward engine's sounds to make it feel more like a real plane. Soon we reached St. Joseph School.

I was completely mesmerised by the looks and size of the building. I had never seen anything as giant as that. If Bihari version of 'Harry Potter' would have been shot in Sitamarhi, I am sure that school would have been pictured as Hogwarts. Papa and I entered principal's chamber. After having a small chat with Father Malcolm, papa told me to stay there for few hours. He also promised he would come back and take me home. I was perfectly alright. Father Malcolm escorted me to my

'Baby Class' and introduced me to fellow kids. Few of them were clapping, few were staring at me and rest of them were damn busy in their works. Somehow I managed to get a seat for myself in the corner of the class.

After few hours, papa came and took me back to home. I still had all of the toffees in my bag as I made no friends on my very first day in the school. Anyway, days kept on passing and I settled myself into that environment. Everyday teacher would play silly games with us, ask us to perform a dance or recite a poem and after that tell us to open our lunch boxes and have our lunch. Everyone would share their lunch but I always preferred having all my meal myself without giving it to anyone or taking anything from anybody. Almost 10 months had passed following the same routine. By that time, it seemed to me that schools were just about spending some time with a bunch of creepy kids and most importantly, eating your lunch. I was never taught anything by anybody in those 10 months. That's what 'Baby Class' is all about; all play and no work! Soon I was promoted to L.K.G. and then to the U.K.G.

I remembered my school prayer, pledge, Carols and participated in a dance and fancy dress competition. Almost everything remained same inside the class except for the study part. Now there were English, mathematics, G.K., science and Hindi periods. I started enjoying those classes as half of the syllabus was already covered by me. All thanks to mommy and home-schooling. I also realised the joy of knowing things in advance in class.

Three years had passed. Grandpa had decided to put me in another school which was nearby home as compared to St. Joseph. I too got to know about that school change thing. But there was nothing I could do or say as I knew grandpa would never take a decision without thinking deeply. On my last day in the school, I distributed chocolates among all my classmates. That day I made so many friends over there. Sadly, I don't remember any of them now. I would have taken their mobile numbers or e-mail addresses but I couldn't, as internet and mobiles were not there in Sitamarhi back then. Though I have with me a photograph of that fancy dress competition yet I am unable to recognise or remember anyone in it except myself. I was all set to raid another school…

5

LIFE AT N.S.D.A.V.

It was March of 1998 when I turned six and got my admission in N.S.D.A.V. Public School, Dumra, Sitamarhi. That school had two different sites named Old Building and New Building. Old building had classes till fourth grade and new building had classes from fifth grade through 12th grade. D.A.V. was even bigger than St. Joseph's. I cleared an easy admission test and got direct admission into second grade and bypassing grade 1st. I spent initial days in that school sitting in the corner of the classroom. I used to be very reserved and introvert. I would only reply to those who initiate conversation with me at the first place. Eventually, I made some very good friends. Though we separated through the course of time, yet we have each other in our hearts and memories. My school life would not have been this much interesting and memorable without some of these folks. I cherish each and every moment spent with them in school and hope they still (at least) remember me.

My very first friend in D.A.V. was Sheetal. He was a very simple and bright student back then. He would always assist me with my homework and assignments. Each day he would bring lunch for me as well; perhaps that's the reason why he was my good friend, initially! We used to sit together, always. Together we would often pass funny comments on other not-so-cool classmates. We had many similarities between us. Being reserved and focused was one of those similarities. All these things made our bond stronger day by day. After two years we just got Separated as he was put into another Section. Mine was last roll number in section A and his was first roll number in section B. I don't have his phone number but we are still on each other's Facebook friends list. Also, I still remember the taste of that 'Aloo Gobi' (cauliflower and potatoes) which he used to bring for lunch.

Another friend of mine was Shubhendu Abhishek. He too was very bright in studies. Shubhendu had a macho personality that helped him attract more and more girls towards himself. He used to call me 'Garam Masala' as I would call him 'Mango Shake' (it rhymes with Abhishek). Upon asking him about his goal of life he always used to say he wants to be the Air Chief Marshal of India. However, today he works at Shipping Corporation of India as he pursued his studies in engineering (merchant navy) from MERI, Kolkata. He has developed a flair for writing. Though we talk to each other occasionally yet we remember those good old days spent together.

When it comes to friendship I simply cannot forget to talk about Vivek. Among all my friends in D.A.V., Vivek was very much like me. He was reserved in nature, bright in academics, sensible and humorous as well. We used to sit together on the same desk. We often crack jokes in class, poke others, pass on funny comments and attend almost every class (at least physically!). Vivek's sister Nidhi was also in our school. Though we used to meet with each other quite often (co-incidentally) in school premises yet we did not have much to talk about. I and Nidhi share our birthdays. Vivek studied at Tolani Maritime Institute and now works for Maersk Line as Assistant Engineer Officer.

We all have that one friend who loves sports more than anything else. I too had one friend. His name was Kedar. He was lean, tall and very much enthusiastic about outdoor sports. Whenever we had our games period in school, Kedar was the first one to run towards the playground. He used to participate in each and every sports competition held in the school. It seemed obvious that he would make his career in sports. But I was shocked when I found that he studied hotel management from IHM, Shimla.

Nikesh and Sushil were another two musketeers in my class. Nikesh was neither very bright in studies nor he had any remarkable interest in sports. But he always lived his school life to its fullest. He had an ability to extract joy out of every common situation in life. Sushil, on the other hand, was even worse in studies. He hardly managed to pass in each subject. But one could not simply ignore his presence in class. He had an influence on all of us. All of the boys in my class would go crazy if Sushil would not come to school for one day. After all, we were very much addicted to his 'non-veg' jokes. He would easily crack a joke out of nothing and make us laugh like anything. I am still in touch with Nikesh, however, Sushil and I never talked after I left my school.

Perhaps, the only friend of mine who went to IIT was Saurav. He pursued Mining Engineering from IIT Kharagpur. From the very beginning, I was sure that Saurav would do something impressive in his career. He was very focused in class and would be easily upset with his slightly low performance in any of the subjects.

One friend that was close to my heart was Mrigendra. We used to go to school together on a school bus. He resided near my shop. I often visit his home to play or study. His mother and grand-mother would love me enormously. I still talk to him once every month.

Prashant, Harish and Avinash were some of my friends from other sections. I clearly remember Avinash bringing his grandpa every time he had some issues with school management. Prashant was more mature as compared to any other student. While Harish did not give a damn about anything except studies. Now Prashant is pursuing his Master's in Industrial Engineering from the University of Texas, Arlington Campus, USA. We both are in touch now.

Those were times when co-education was not that popular in schools of Bihar. Most of the schools were either boys' or girls' schools. Though some prominent institutions like D.A.V. and St. Joseph had adopted co-ed fashion yet it was affected with a little conservationism. Boys and girls would sit apart on separate desks. It seems quite old-fashioned if I look back in time but those distances, conserved behaviour and shyness had its own fun. Boys used to consider themselves lucky if a girl simply drank water from their water bottle. While for girls it was a matter of diffidence if a boy asked for her pen or pencil. I always liked to be reserved in my school days. Even after not socialising enthusiastically, I made some friends; and they were girls. I remember some of them as if I left D.A.V. yesterday. Perhaps my connectivity with them on Facebook is the reason why I feel them in proximity.

Shraddha, Khushboo, Heena and Ankita are those friends of whom I see updates via FB. Shraddha used to be one of the simplest girls in my class. She believed in living life to its fullest. Though she was light hearted yet she took every responsibility seriously. Once, Shraddha was caught by Verma Sir during class. She was talking to Kritika while Verma Sir was teaching some shit related to space and matter. Those were the times when talking while class is going on was a bigger crime than murdering someone. Verma Sir scolded Shraddha and asked the reason behind the talk. The exact conversation was as follows:

Verma Sir (angry): Why were you talking? Hmm…Now tell me, what's the matter (between both of you)?

Shraddha (frightened): Anything that occupies space and has mass is called matter.

And we all started laughing like anything. That was the first time I ever saw Verma Sir laughing. It took some time for Shraddha to understand what went wrong. After realising the humour in that situation she too had a decent smile on her face. She looked beautiful. I fell in love with her at an age when I did not even know what love was all about, I confess. I could not gather the courage to approach her and tell about my feelings. Had I been bold enough to convey how I felt for her, I would have a different present in all likelihood. She has completed her masters. She is wiser than what she was in school and has become even more beautiful now.

Khushboo was very much interested in indoor and outdoor sports. She was taller than most of the boys in my class. She had a remarkable interest in table tennis, football, badminton and Kho-kho. Heena, on the other hand, was subtle in nature. She had a little bit of everything in her. Her gentle smile would make anybody do anything for her.

Almost every class has so called 'elite' group of girls who consider themselves as Rapunzel(s). I too had such a group in my class. This group had a trio of girls namely Shubhra, Medha and Amrit. Shubhra and Medha were good in academics. However, Amrit was inclined towards dancing and acting. I have not been in touch with them since I left my school.

Through ups and downs, peaks and valleys, I learned to excel. I miss all my teachers who genuinely guided me throughout my school life. That fear when we used to forget to do our homework given by Tripathi Sir, that fun we used to have in class with A.K. Mishra Sir and that seriousness when

Prasad Sir used to scold the entire class…is irreplaceable.Things have changed a lot. We all got engaged with our careers. With the course of time friendship changed its dimensions. Today, we rarely say 'Hi' to each other. That does not mean we forgot each other or no longer want to talk to each other. It's just that we are busy making our lives better and even better. My life in D.A.V. was full of surprises, joys, sorrows and inspirations. It showed me many aspects of life. I cherish each and every day spent in D.A.V. I left this school after completing grade 9th in 2006.

6

SEE YOU! MOMMY

Sitamarhi had been witnessing heavy flooding since ages. Heavy rainfall and excessive water discharge from dams in Nepal are the reasons behind this catastrophe. Every time it floods in the city it causes extreme devastation to agriculture, transit, electricity and infrastructure. Like all other business, ours too would suffer from this catastrophe every year. As soon as we would recover from the damage caused by last year's flood we found ourselves trapped within the next one.

In the year 2004 when our town was affected by the flood, I experienced what it is like being in the middle of nowhere. The whole town was cut-off from major cities like Patna and Muzaffarpur. Sitamarhi turned into an isolated island with no communication, no transportation, no electricity and no supplies/groceries for two weeks. Imagine days and nights where you have nowhere to go, all dark everywhere, nothing to do and nothing to eat. You have 3 feet of dirty muddy water inside your house all over, and not only that, you witness all kinds of creepy water animals like snakes, crabs, frogs, and fishes swimming around your bed. You are sleepless since past three days not because you have these creatures around you but because you never know when water level will rise and you will find yourself swimming with these animals in the darkness of hollow night. I have lived this situation when I was 12.

That garden in which I used to play with grandpa was completely collapsed. Though floods have always been scary for me on one hand while on the other hand I was not disturbed this time as I knew it would not last forever. And moreover, I was happy because I did not have to go school for an undetermined period of time. I had no idea what my family was going through. Grandpa and papa were in deep trouble. They had nothing to do and were worried about our survival. My family was on the brink of bankruptcy. Grandpa estimated that we had limited financial resources which were supposed to support us for a month only. And it would take almost six months to get everything back on track. Fortunately, the city and its services were restored fully within two months.

After witnessing that terrible disaster grandpa and papa took an important decision that was about to change my life along with my family's. They decided to leave Sitamarhi and move to Delhi permanently. I was not informed of this decision immediately. Time passed and I continued my studies. It was good to see my school friends after such a long time. Two months after school was reopened, I took my board exam. D.A.V. had its own board exam for grade eighth at that time. Somehow I managed to pass that exam and was promoted to ninth grade.

Since my family had decided to leave Sitamarhi and move to Delhi permanently, we began to plan our packing and moving. There were many factors which were considered at that time. The top-most priority was my studies. It was clear that grandpa would not let my studies hamper by this decision. So, everybody decided that mommy and little brother would leave first. They had to arrange for an accommodation in Delhi. My younger brother was supposed to get admission in fifth grade in Delhi. Then Chachu along with his family would leave after selling our business and all its merchandises. Then papa would leave as he would look for setting up a business or taking a job in Delhi.

I along with my grandpa and grandma will leave at last after grandpa arranges for a buyer for our house in Sitamarhi. Meanwhile, I would pursue my studies in D.A.V. until I pass grade ninth.

After we all agreed to this plan mommy and brother got their tickets booked for Delhi. They had to leave in about one month and a half. Initially, they had to stay at maternal grandpa's house, which was no less than a castle! In a blink of an eye, that day had come when mommy and brother were all set to go to the station. They had their train from Muzaffarpur Junction. Papa and I went along with them to the station. It takes almost two hours from Sitamarhi to reach Muzaffarpur by bus. We grabbed our seats on the side where four seats were aligned together. Brother started asking for a window seat. Usually, windows seats were supposed to be meant for me. But I did not make any fuss and let him sit on the window side.

That day, the bus driver had played a Hollywood movie dubbed in Hindi. Perhaps this was the very first time I could not focus on the movie while travelling by Bihar State Road Transportation Corporation's bus. May be because I was little worried and upset as I would not see mommy and brother for a long time.Through crest and trough of 'Kutcha' roads of Bihar, our ramshackle bus reached Muzaffarpur Railway Station. The station had not changed at all in so many years. I witnessed stinky coolies (baggage handlers), dirty walls, loud announcements and exodus of people moving here and there at the station platforms. As our move to Delhi was final and permanent, mommy had a lot of luggage with herself. Papa hired two coolies and we proceeded towards platform 14. Since railway stations were packed with crowd those days, it was quite a challenge for parents to watch their kids and keep an eye on coolie simultaneously at stations.

We reached platform 14 finally after making our way through the ginormous crowd. After few minutes, the train arrived at the platform. It was simply humongous, seemed like a red dragon (trains have been painted blue now but they were red those days). People were quickly boarding and de-boarding the train. Everything started to seem slow to me. Things appeared to be fading as I was about to lose my patience and start crying. I could feel the warmth of tear drops scrolling down on my cheeks. Mommy hugged and told me to focus on my studies. I touched her feet to seek blessings. Brother was smiling as he was too small and innocent to understand the situation. Before I or mommy could say something to each other, we heard the very strong sound of a train whistle. In seconds, the train started to crawl. Mommy and brother rapidly got inside and grabbed their reserved seats. Brother started waving at me and papa. I too waved with a smile and they gradually disappeared from my line of sight. I and papa stood there until train crossed the entire length of the platform.

After exiting the station premises papa bought a pack of 'Uncle Chips' and a bottle of 'Frooti' for me. I was not that excited this time as I usually used to be after getting a pack of chips and Frooti. There was a feeling of loss inside my heart, or rather the loss of feeling inside my mind, I am not sure.We boarded the same bus in which we had arrived at the station. The same bus was going back to Sitamarhi carrying even more passengers. I and papa got our seats. I sat on window seat as I did not want to watch that creepily dubbed movie bus driver had played. Moreover, brother was not there anymore to demand for a window seat. I was not at my peace. I don't remember my journey on that bus as I fell asleep. What I remember is papa waking me up at Sitamarhi bus terminal. We reached home and I had dinner with everyone. Dinner was quiet, devoid of any noise that night. Since I was really exhausted physically as well as mentally, I went to bed hoping for a new, light start for my remaining days in Sitamarhi. A tiring day ended as I fell asleep soon.

7

Last Year in Sitamarhi

Next morning, I woke up early, at around 6 AM. I looked beside me and saw a wide gap between myself and where papa was sleeping. I then remembered within a second that mommy and brother are gone now, therefore it was only I and papa in the room. I pacified my heart and gathered the courage to lead my life without mom and brother. I had to go to school that day. I came out of my room swiftly. I saw grandpa was ready to go into the garden and grandma was preparing tea for grandpa and herself. Had mommy been there, she would have prepared that morning tea for everybody. But seeing grandma in the kitchen was a different kind of delight. I knew I will have food prepared by grandma. I loved the way grandma used to cook food in her style. Though mommy was an expert in kitchen affairs, yet grandma had her own legacy when it came to food and cuisine.

After an hour or so, papa woke up. I reminded him to call Delhi (Nana Ji's house) so as to confirm mommy's and brother's arrival. By that time, we had done away with landline phone as we were moving out permanently and mobile phones were not yet popularly introduced in Bihar (or anywhere in India, I guess). Papa went to a nearby PCO booth to make that phone call. That booth was owned by Shankar, a helpful guy. I clearly remember those big banners saying 'Shankar Booth: STD, ISD & PCO'. Meanwhile, I started to get ready for my school. Papa soon returned and told us about mommy's safe arrival & he went to open the shop. Luckily, the train was on time and Mamu came to receive them at New Delhi Railway Station. Grandma packed my lunch and gave one paratha to me for my breakfast. I ate that paratha which tasted utterly delicious. Grandpa also got ready to go to the temple. I used to board my school bus at 8 AM sharp. Every day, while eating my breakfast I would watch Pokémon on Cartoon Network. That day, I and grandpa left together. I stopped at my bus stop while grandpa kept walking towards the temple, which was a little ahead from where I was standing. I could see him offering Prasad and water upon Shiva-Lingam. My bus arrived and I boarded the bus. Grandpa and I waved each other. The bus driver saw grandpa and made a greeting gesture to him. Grandpa in return smiled and accepted that greeting from the driver. This is the beauty of living in a small town where everyone knows you and you know everyone. There is a sense of belongingness and association among people. You get respect and in return, you give respect to fellow citizens. Despite having ideological differences among them, people of Sitamarhi held the spirit of brotherhood in their hearts.

Anyways, time flies and it flies quickly. After about three months and a half, papa had sold almost everything in our shop. The shop had nothing much to offer. However, there were some small merchandises left to be sold. Also, there were some people rather long-time loyal customers in the industry who owed us some decent amount of money as we had monthly register for them. They used to pay us every month for the goods they purchased during respective month. Business used to run on mutual trust then. Since business was almost closed papa and chachu decided to leave. One fine afternoon, while on my bus returning to home from school, I saw my shop closed. It was quite a shock for me as I in my entire life had never seen my shop closed in the afternoon. Either papa or chachu or grandpa has to be in the shop. I decided to get off from the bus right there, right then. I wanted to go there and see what had happened. But then I realised there was nothing I could do after getting off from the bus. The shop was already closed, I had no phone and there was nobody known to me nearby the shop. So I decided to go home first and see what the matter was.

After I reached home I found that both papa and chachu (along with chachi) were packing their suitcases and bags. I asked them in anxiety where they were going. I got to know that they had their train for Delhi that evening. It was so sudden for me that it took few minutes for me to believe that. I was sad; really sad after hearing that.While I was eating my lunch with grandma, papa came out of his room dragging two big suitcases along with him. He called chachu and reminded the time of the train departure from Patna Junction. It was a 5 hour's journey from Sitamarhi to Patna by bus those days. By the time I finished eating my meal, everyone was ready with their luggage to leave for Patna. I too wanted to go with them to see them off but I could not as there wasn't anybody I could come back with to Sitamarhi. I remember grandma asking them to keep their dinner with them, grandpa asking papa to have some cash with him, papa confirming with chachu whether he kept the train ticket or not and chachi filling water camphor.

Meanwhile in the midst of these last minute conversations, I felt a heavy thrust inside my heart. It was an uneasy feeling which was making me shallow. I could not control this time and started crying vigorously. Everybody stopped doing whatever they were doing and started placating me. Papa assured that soon I too will be with them once I complete grade ninth. I had no other option but to believe that soon our family will be together. With that hope in my mind, I somehow stopped crying and touched their feet to seek blessings.

Soon there was a knock on our door. It was our family Rickshaw-puller who was waiting since past 15 minutes or so to drop them to the Sitamarhi bus terminal. Before leaving, papa made sure that Shankar, the phone booth guy communicates every message from them to us and vice-versa. I remember chachu giving me a 50-rupee note and instructed me to spend it wisely. Getting a 50-rupee note was quite a big deal for kids those days and that too in a town like Sitamarhi. I could buy an entire world with those 50 rupees. Anyways, I kept standing at my door waving until I could not see them anymore. I realised only three of us were left behind. I also discovered that a home is not a home without its people living, enjoying, and experiencing every joy and sorrow together. Without them home becomes a house, a house which is mere an infrastructure with a roof, walls and windows and nothing else.

A few hours later Shankar came to the home and told us about the call papa made to him from the station so as we know that they have arrived Patna safely. That night grandma asked me what I wanted to eat for dinner. I had no idea what to say. Even I had no idea if I really wanted to eat something or not. I said her I did not want to eat. Prior to this date, there was not a single day when I said no to my dinner. Grandma knew I was not in a mood to do anything or to eat or to talk. She hugged me and made me understand the gravity of the situation. Also, she made me think of our future in which everything was going to be alright. I was mature enough to understand those circumstances. My brain was aware that we all would be together soon but my heart seemed shaken a bit. She then asked me again for dinner and insisted nobody will eat if I would not eat. I then made myself understand the very nature of life and said yes for the dinner. Grandpa switched on his transistor (a radio that operates on Amplitude Modulation). We could hear All India Radio's news bulletin very clearly. It was eight in the evening. We ate our dinner together. It was very silent and quick dinner that night. A table where eight people used to eat together since the very beginning was now having five chairs vacant all of a sudden. That big mansion which was equipped with the then modern amenities became less important, my own home slowly started to become a strange place to me.

Next morning grandma wakes me up. I had my school that day. Initially, I did not want to go to school. But then somehow I realised I am not doing any good to anybody by not going to school. Therefore, I got up, took a shower and ate my breakfast while watching Pokémon. Meanwhile, grandpa returned from the temple. He offered me, Prasad. I was about to say no to him but then I realised it is not the right item to say no to. I was told many times before that we should never say no to Prasad as it is not just something sweet to eat but it is the blessings of the almighty. Even before I could think of taking it with one hand, grandpa commanded me to take the Prasad with both of my hands. A typical Brahmin family, I told you!

Since it was only grandpa who had to take care of the shop, he left without having his breakfast. Grandma used to tell him every now and then not to worry about the shop anymore. But grandpa had started that business, he had seen it flourishing and hence, he developed a love for his work. He could not simply leave everything all at once.

Time passed by quickly and six months were gone in a blink of an eye. I was mid-way through my grade ninth studies. By that time mommy, brother, papa, chachu and chachi were settled in Delhi. They had found a decent accommodation on rent and brother had got his admission in fifth grade in a small school nearby. Papa and chachu had figured out their new field of occupation. Chachu decided to go for a private service. Hence he went for motor (car) servicing and insurance claim industry. Based on his prior experience and knowledge he was appointed as a Service Advisor in MGF Hyundai, West Delhi. Whereas papa joined Phupha ji in his family business.

And here was I in Sitamarhi, still following my same daily routine of getting up in the morning, working sometimes in the garden with grandpa, taking a shower, eating breakfast while watching TV, leaving for school, spend some time in school and then come back home. One thing that had changed during this period was my TV schedule. Now I could watch Pokémon and Digi-Môn one after another on Cartoon Network before leaving for the school. Another thing that had changed significantly was the way we were taught in the school. Since grade ninth was considered fairly senior class in my school, we were treated as seniors. All our subject teachers started being more liberal and lenient towards us. We used to have quizzes, outdoor and indoor games and plays more often. One of my favourite trends was playing Dumb Charades in class. All we had to do was put some emotional pressure and request our teachers 'N' number of times. They all used to agree most of the times. The whole class would be divided into two groups. Each group would have a mixture of girls and boys.

Things were changing and our mentality too. The concept of co-education was being fully exercised in schools of Bihar. It was not just about having girls and boys in the same class, but it was about sharing, interacting and enjoying each other's company. So, I, Vivek, Shubhendu, Kedar, Prashant, Shraddha, Heena, Ankita, and Khushboo used to be on the same side along with some of our classmates. And Nikesh, Sushil, Saurav, Shubhra, Medha and Amrit would be on the other side with remaining classmates. We used to have some serious fun in those days. Studies were not left much. It became more of a formality to come to school.

One day I went to my school Principal and told him about my situation at home. I told him I didn't want to come to school anymore because I was done with the studies. We were supposed to have our final exams in three months. Also, I made him understand that I wanted to help grandpa with his routine work at the shop. My school Principal understood my situation and appreciated the fact that I wanted to help grandpa. After all, he too knew that studies were almost over and students come to school just to maintain their attendance and to meet their friends. He finally approved my request and gave me permission to be at home without being penalised for my long term absence from school. Of course, I told him I would come to take my final exams only.

That day after discussing with the Principal, I returned to my class and told all my friends about the reason behind my long term future absence from the school. They all understood and gave a farewell kind of reaction. I then told them I would obviously come to sit in my exams. They all became little optimistic then. That was almost the last day of my school.

I came back home and told everything to grandma and grandpa. Grandma was very happy to hear that. Grandpa, however, showed 'it was not necessary but appreciated' kind of attitude initially. I knew he was thinking of himself to be the reason behind my absence in school. I then told him that school was just becoming a formality those days. Finally, we both came to a common conscience. He then hugged me and appreciated my decision of bearing business responsibility and sharing it with grandpa.

From that day, my sole purpose of living everyday was to help my grandpa as much as I could in wrapping up our business.

Now it was I who would wake up at seven in the morning and go open the shop riding on my bicycle. I would clean, dust and broom the shop. I used to read that 'Hindustan' newspaper daily. Grandpa would then come on rickshaw after an hour or so to the shop. Then I would leave for home. I would take a shower and eat my breakfast, now without watching any TV. Then again I had to leave for the shop. After about three hours later grandpa would go home for his lunch. He would also take a short nap before returning to the shop in the evening. Once he would come to the shop, I was supposed to go for collecting our money from those customers whom we had arranged monthly payment system for. This activity is called 'Tagaada' in colloquial Hindi. It means to remind someone about paying their dues as soon as possible. So while doing tagaada, there were times when I would instantly get money from the customers. But the market was full of shitty people too. Some of them often postpone the payment and would ask me to come next day or next week or even next month! I had to be assertive then. I mean it was my money which they should have paid immediately after taking stuff from my shop. But nobody would take a 13-year-old boy that seriously.

Anyways, I would follow this routine every day. Whenever I would get some money from someone I would be very excited while handing it over to grandpa. Grandpa would then give me five rupees as my reward. I would become more than happy to get that money. At around eight in the evening, grandpa would leave for home. He always had a dry cell torch with him. The condition of electricity in Sitamarhi was not so good. He would always tell me to close the shop fifteen to twenty minutes after he leaves. However, I always used to close the shop at around 10 PM after one of our competitors used to close his shop. I really wanted to sell everything as soon as possible. At around 10 AM I would close all the shutters and lock them up. I would then double check the locks. I would then return back to home on my bicycle. It would take me about ten minutes to reach home on a bicycle. After I reach home, we would have dinner together. Grandma would often cook something sweet for the dessert. I and grandpa loved to have something sweet after eating our meal.

Those three months were highly engaging and memorable for me. I witnessed the harsh reality of doing business. I met so many good and bad people, I learnt the basics of establishing good relations and rapport with people. I then realised what it takes to set up a business in a completely strange place. I then realised what it takes to make a business grow out of nothing. It takes a lot of optimism mixed with courage and dedication wrapped over a vision to be successful. There were times when grandpa would lose his heart and faith in life as his emotional struggle became tough and tougher day by day. Those were the times when I reminded him of something he would always tell me. He would always tell me about an old saying in Urdu, viz. "Himmat-e-Marda, Madad-e-Khuda" (God helps those who have the courage to help themselves). This would then restore his faith in Lord Shiva and he would assure me that everything is going to be alright.

8

Goodbye, Home!

It was March of 2006 when my friend Ravi Shankar visited my home on his bicycle. He came to inform me about our date sheet for final exams. I came to know that in one week I had my final exams and one week after that I would be done with my studies in D.A.V. Public School. Ravi left after having a cup of tea. I decided to study for my exams from the next day. However, I could not get time to study that day, the next day after that day and next to next day after that day as well.

Soon the day came when I had my first exam. It was on March 4th and the day was Saturday and it was my birthday too. I was not even bothered about the exam. In fact, I was feeling a joy inside me. I was happy to think of my freedom once I am done with my schooling in Sitamarhi.

Anyways, I took all my exams and they all went well. Now I was free from the school. However, I had to wait until my results were out as I had to apply for my Transfer Certificate. It was not possible to get admission in any other school without taking my TC from D.A.V. Public. In last week of March, results were declared. I secured good marks (I guess 78%) in my ninth grade. Soon after I got my results, I applied for my Transfer Certificate. It was processed the next day and I was given my migration certificate, character certificate, my transcripts and

TC. I bid farewell to all my friends and teachers. We all friends promised to be in touch by every means possible. Finally, it was my last day in D.A.V. school.

I came back to home and called papa from Shankar's Booth. I had to inform him about my result and that I was ready to come to Delhi. Papa had given us a landline number on which we were supposed to call if we had to talk. It was their landlord's number.

Every time I would call that number a girl would pick up. Then I would ask her to call my brother, Aman from the second floor. She then would shout either 'Puja Aunty', or 'Aman' and then I would get someone from my family to talk with. I had to hold the call for a minute or two while someone from my family comes downstairs. In the meantime, I often used to think about that girl who always picked up my phone at the very first place. I would imagine the anger and rage she had to go over every time she shouts while calling mommy or brother downstairs. I would try to imagine myself in her place. To me, it seemed little irritating to bother or annoy someone for my needs. That day I insisted papa buy a mobile phone for himself so that we all can easily keep in touch without disturbing anybody.

Papa bought a Motorola cell phone with Airtel connection the next day. Soon I got to know the girl who always picked my phone was Leema. I had wondered several times about what kind of name that girl had, Leema (what does that mean? What on earth inspired her parents to give her this name?). I got to know that she was Christian. 'Umm...these people do have these kinds of names.' I satisfied myself with this well-thought-of judgement of mine.

In the first week of April, my Bua came from Chandigarh to visit us in Sitamarhi. She wanted to make sure everything was alright with me, grandpa and grandma. She had come there for four days. Then she suggested grandma send me with her to Chandigarh for one week. It would be a change for me as well. Grandma had no objection. Grandpa even appreciated her idea. Grandma was already eager to send me as soon as possible because people had already known about our permanent move to Delhi. Since, grandpa had found a buyer and we had to sell our house and shop we were supposed to get a lot of money from that. This sudden inflow of money could motivate some bad elements of the society to harm us (me specifically) so as to take that money from us.

Those were the times when kidnapping was a trending crime in Bihar. This created a fear inside grandma's mind and she immediately decided to send me to Chandigarh with Bua. Even I knew some or the other day it was going to happen. We all had to leave Sitamarhi. So why not now? I thought. Two days after it was decided that I must go with Bua, I got my reservations done in 'Tatkal' quota.

Next day, I, Bua and Vasu (my cousin) had our train at around 9.15 AM to Chandigarh from Muzaffarpur Junction. I felt an emotional imbalance inside my mind. I was going through a series of continuous impulses. I started to collect all my stuff including my documents, clothes, some gadgets, and even my toothbrush to pack it in a suitcase. I could not figure out what all should I take along with me and what all to be left there forever. Grandma helped me in packing my stuff. In a wick of second darkness gulped over the day. Bua lit the lantern. Grandma lit another lantern and hung it on the lantern stand. I could hear the sound of mosquitoes flying all over. Grandpa asked me to use mosquito repellent coil, which was popularly known as 'Katchua Chhap'. As soon as I did that our house became mosquito-free. I liked the incense of that katchua chhap coils. However, mosquitoes hated that thing as it would suffocate them. That day Bua and grandma prepared dinner. Bua cooked more than what was required for the dinner and I wondered why. Grandpa turned on his transistor, we ate dinner, had some chit-chat and slept as we had to leave very early next morning.

I remember Bua waking me up next morning. With both of my eyes still closed, I heard her waking up Vasu and saying we would miss our train if he would not get up instantly. This banged inside my head and I realised we had to leave early.

Since it would take almost two and half hours to reach Muzaffarpur, we had to leave from home by 6 AM latest. I just removed whatever the hell was above me (it was a sheet though) and left my bed. I stood up quickly and went outside my room to see what everyone else was doing. I was the last person to wake up that day. There was a chaos in my house. Everybody was in a rush. Bua was reheating the food, grandma was giving a towel to Vasu as he was going to take a bath, grandpa was in the garden and I was still rubbing my eyes and trying to figure out what to do. Then Bua said *'jaldi karle'* (hurry up) or else we would miss the train. I thought what do I do *jaldi* (quickly)?

Anyways, I took a shower as soon as my cousin came out of the bathroom. It was still a little dark outside as it was pretty early in the morning. We were all set to leave. Our rickshaw-puller had already arrived so as to drop us at the bus terminal. This time, I had nothing inside my mind. I felt a loss of feeling. I hugged grandma and touched her feet. Then I touched grandpa's feet. 'We are coming right after you', said grandpa, while smiling. 'See you soon in Delhi', I said. And we hopped on that rickshaw. Nobody except my family knew that I was leaving that day. That was my last day in Sitamarhi. It was not easy for me to leave that place where I had grown up. I was born in Delhi but spent my childhood in Sitamarhi. Even after spending my days and nights in complete darkness, despite combating with tonnes of mosquitoes every single night, studying in the dim light of kerosene lamps, struggling every time I rode my bicycle on kutcha roads and witnessing catastrophic floods several times, I loved being there in Sitamarhi.

That joy when I would see my fan running after two days or so, that relief I used to feel after making my house mosquito-free with 'katchua chhap coils' and that dedication of studying in the dim light of the lamps were incredible. Those bumps on the road which made me lose my balance several times ultimately made me a pro in bicycle-riding. Those close encounters with creatures like goats, bulls, cows, buffaloes, lizards, houseflies, cockroaches, snails and snakes made me love Mother Nature. I embrace its history, the peace in the atmosphere, harmony, brotherhood in people and those imbalances in civic patterns of the society which made Sitamarhi a remarkable place to live.

9

Enroute Chandigarh

We reached Sitamarhi bus terminal and waited for the right bus which would take us all the way to Muzaffarpur railway station. I grabbed the aisle seat as this time I wanted to watch the movie. I was happy to think of my future where I and my family members would be together. Since the beginning of my life, I had grown up in a joint family. Living in a nuclear family was something unimaginable for me.

The bus started to move slowly. The conductor was shouting 'Runni-Saidpur, Muzaffarpur, Patna' so as to pack as many passengers as he could into that bus. Some people were sitting on the bus as there was no standing space left inside it. I did not mind the crowd as I was sitting comfortably in my seat. I could view the TV very clearly. It was a movie starring Govinda and Karishma Kapoor. Those were the times when actors like Govinda, Karishma Kapoor, Ravina Tandon and Sunil Shetty were at the peak of their Bollywood career. Every single movie had to have these stars in it.The movie was entertaining and we reached the station soon after that movie ended. We let fellow passengers get off the bus first. Then Bua grabbed two bags, Vasu held one suitcase and I grabbed my suitcase and another bag which had water, food and some other stuff. We quickly walked towards the station. It was almost nine in the morning and sun has risen to its fullest. I could barely see any other bus parked at the station. As soon as we entered station premises a group of coolies wearing red shirt approached towards us. They all were insisting upon handing over our luggage to them. They had just started their day, I presumed. However, Bua said no to each and every coolie. Within minutes we were on platform number 10. We had waited there for about fifteen minutes. In those fifteen minutes, I heard only two kinds of announcements several times. One had 'the inconvenience caused is deeply regretted' in their last note as these were the announcements confirming the late arrival of the trains whereas another announcement was for an old lady who was separated from her family at the station.

The train arrived at right time and we entered our compartment. It was an AC car. That was the first time I saw Air Conditioned car of Indian Railways. Although it looked same as a normal car, yet it had a different feel and atmosphere. It was well maintained, covered and had curtains, pillow and bedsheets as well. People were also seemed to be more sophisticated than those who would get their reservations done in a sleeper car. I was amazed at the cooling capacity of that car. I praised Railways inside my mind. That 'good for nothing' image of railways inside my mind had turned upside down. By that time trains were painted in blue colour. I dragged all our luggage under the berth and made sure nothing was left unattended.

The train crawled after some time. I could see people moving here and there outside from sealed sun-ban glass windows but nobody from outside could see me. I looked at Bua's face and she smiled. Vasu asked me how I was feeling. 'I am good and want to reach as soon as possible', I replied. Meanwhile, IRCTC vendors started selling their drinks and snacks in the train. Bua bought a cup of tea for herself. I was feeling sleepy by then. I told her that I was going to get some sleep. She suggested me to go to the upper berth and sleep. I climbed up to the berth and laid down. As the train was moving pretty fast, I was feeling slight thumps generated by its motion. It was a relaxing combination and I fell asleep. I slept almost for the entire day. I guess it was my hunger which woke me up. I asked Bua for some food and what I had in front of me was exactly same as what I ate last night for dinner. Then I realised the reason why Bua was cooking more food than it was supposed to be cooked for dinner last night. Things happen for a reason.

Very soon it was 10 in the night. Almost everybody in my compartment was in deep slumber. Those who were awake were eating their dinner. Bua and Vasu were on their respective berths but yet not slept. We were supposed to reach at six in the morning. After sometime I peeped down from upper berth and saw everybody was sleeping. It was only me who was acting like a night owl in that car. What could I have done, I could not sleep as I had already slept for an entire day. I was awake the whole night. Some Train Ticket Examiners, Chai-Wala, passengers, railway police officials and vendors kept on passing through my compartment whole night. All I could do was stare at them and then at my luggage which was beneath the berth. It was hard to figure out which bag was which but still I could make sure that something is there.

Theft was a common incident in trains, especially trains from Bihar and U.P. those days. People were likely to lose their luggage while travelling in trains. That was the reason why most of the passengers used to purchase a chain and lock to tie their luggage with seat handle. Well, it all depends on your luck, it depends on what type of thief you are encountering with. Some were really pro in what they used to do. They would even break the lock and steal your baggage along with the chain you had purchased to protect the bag. Stealing is really an art, a dangerous, risky art, though.

We reached Ambala station where the train was scheduled to stop for at least 15 minutes. I went down my berth and asked if Bua or Vasu wanted anything from outside. They simply denied. Then I got off from the train and stretched. I felt refreshing that morning. It was a little cold morning. People were getting off to fill their water bottles, some were buying 'Chhole-Kulche' and 'Aloo-Puri' to eat.

Fifteen minutes passed very quickly and all those who got off from the train started getting on quickly. I too quickly got inside. The train whistled three times and moved with a bump. I did not go to upper berth as it takes less than half an hour to reach Chandigarh from Ambala station. I sat beside Vasu. Almost half of the train got empty at Ambala station. Remaining were supposed to de-board at Chandigarh. We started collecting and sorting our baggage. Vasu put on his shoes, I did not need to worry about that as I was wearing a pair of *'chappals'* (slippers).

Phupha ji was supposed to receive us at the station. Our train arrived at Chandigarh station finally. I saw phupha ji standing on the platform and waved at him. He too saw me and started walking in the direction of my car. The train was still not stopped and was crawling slowly. Once it had stopped finally, we let fellow passengers debark first. I wondered why people are always in such a hurry. As soon as train or bus stops they all become restless and create a panic to get out from that bus or train. I wondered if people do the same when they get off from the plane or cruise. I would not know as I had never travelled with airlines or ships. I missed my cycle then. In Sitamarhi bicycle was the only mode of transportation for me. I loved riding my bike. Though it was not as fancy as today's cycle yet it was tough on performance. Moreover, it was there even before my birth. Grandpa bought it when he established the business there.

Phupha ji got inside the train. I and Vasu touched his feet. He too hugged both of us and grabbed two of our bags. We then followed him and exit the station. While crossing platforms via a bridge I noticed the serenity at Chandigarh station. There was only one train (ours) at the station. Unlike Muzaffarpur junction where there were 14 platforms, Chandigarh had only four. We sat in his car and within minutes reached home.

10

THE CITY BEAUTIFUL

Bua's home was a fancy duplex in Sector 17 of Chandigarh. It was situated beside Himalaya Marg, a posh colony of the city. It was for the first time I visited Chandigarh. Before that, I had only heard about this city. It was no less than a foreign place to me and no wonder why it is known as the planned city. Despite its beauty and cleanliness, I did not feel that peace of mind in Chandigarh that I used to experience in my town, Sitamarhi. Probably it was all in my mind only. I met Vasu's friends. We all used to play in a park that was well maintained. Every evening we would play football, kabaddi and sometimes cricket together.

Though I enjoyed a lot there yet I had a restlessness inside me of going to Delhi. It had been three days since I came to Chandigarh and I had seen nothing special there. Then, Bua planned a trip to Sukhna Lake and Pinjore Gardens next day. That day was the best day of my time spent in Chandigarh. We did boating, clicked many pictures together, ate a lot of street food and enjoyed. On my way to Pinjore Gardens, I booked my train ticket for Delhi. Now there was a facility to book a train ticket online. I asked for Bua's cell phone and did it myself. I knew Bua will not allow me to leave so early. They wanted me to stay for a longer period of time. That is why I first booked the ticket and then told them about it.

As we middle class people cannot afford to waste our hard earned money, Bua and Phupha ji had no other option left but to agree with me and let me go. Phupha ji did not appreciate this act of mine initially, I promised him I would visit them again soon and he was alright. It hardly takes four hours from Delhi to reach Chandigarh; therefore, I could visit them quite often.

I had my train next day. It was a newly introduced train from New Delhi to Chandigarh named 'Chandigarh Janshatabdi Express'. In just a bit the day had arrived when I was all set to leave from Bua's place for Delhi. I asked Phupha ji if I could drive their scooter from home to the station. Though I did not have a driving license yet I had learned to drive scooter and motorbike with my friends in Sitamarhi. Moreover, I had mastered the art of balancing bicycle. The station was about five minutes from their home. Also, I reminded him that we live in India, so no big deal if I drive without a license. Considering all these factors phupha ji could not deny and we both left for the station.

After about ten minutes we reached there. I parked the scooter and hugged him. He commanded me to keep visiting them on a regular basis. I nodded in affirmative. Then I went inside the station. The train was already there on platform number one.Though I had plenty of time left with me yet I ran towards the train to get to my seat so that I could place my suitcase without any hassle. Mine was a window seat. A lady arrived and requested me politely to exchange my window seat with her middle seat. She was very calm and smiling at me. Had it been anybody else instead of me, he/she would have simply exchanged the seat. Well…I did not give a fuck and said no to her. She got pissed off. Who cares! All her calmness and smile took a dive upside down. It was funny to see that change in her attitude.

I had no idea how time went by. As my train reached Sabzi Mandi station, I knew I am inside Delhi's territory. New Delhi Railway Station is merely five minutes from that station. I felt butterflies in my stomach. I was pretty excited to know that papa would come there to take me home. The train started to slide slowly and kept moving at a snail's pace till it reached New Delhi Station. I was ready with my suitcase in the very front of the line. That moment I realised why people are always in a hurry to get off from bus or train. Probably they have some important work to do or they have their own reasons as I had that day to be in such a hurry. I realised that no teacher is greater than life itself for it teaches us throughout our lives.

11

AM I REALLY IN DELHI?

I saw papa before he could see me. He was looking for me in opposite direction as I forgot to tell him my coach number. I approached him from behind and instantly touched his feet. *'Pairi paina Papa Ji',* (I seek your blessings, father) I said. *'Arre! Beta, khush rahiye!'* (Oh Son! stay blessed) he replied with an ear to ear smile on his face. He was equally delighted to see me as I was to see him after almost one year. He then hugged me and asked me about my journey and about everybody in Chandigarh. Before I could answer him, he continued with asking about how grandpa and grandma were in Sitamarhi. I told him my journey was not bad and everyone was good in Chandigarh and Sitamarhi.

He grabbed my suitcase but I took it from him and insisted on carrying it myself. We exit the station and proceeded towards bus stand. Delhi station seemed very much changed as compared to what it used to be earlier during my visits to Nana Ji's house in Delhi in my summer vacations. There was a huge number of people roaming here and there at the station, the sun was burning the city, the number of taxis, auto-rickshaws, and rickshaws increased heavily and the station was renovated.

We stood near a water vending machine as it had a big umbrella surmounted over. That protected us from the direct sun rays. Meanwhile, papa asked me if I wanted to drink 'Nimbu Pani' (lemonade). I refused but he did not bother to listen to me and anyway brought two glasses, one for each of us. It tickled my taste buds and I quickly sipped all of it. I even finished it before papa could drink it all. He then made me realise the irony of the situation and we both laughed like anything. The bus came with a sign 'RL-77' on it. Everyone got off from the bus as it was the terminal station. Papa asked bus driver about the time he would start the bus for next trip. We got to know that it was ready to go again. What was the wait then, I grabbed a seat and kept one for papa while he was purchasing the tickets. Buses in Delhi were operated by Delhi Transport Corporation. It is the world's largest CNG operated bus service. There were fewer people in that bus as compared to buses in Sitamarhi. Probably because DTC had so many buses running all across the city on a frequent basis while Sitamarhi had inter-city buses only. Also, there were two doors in the bus, front one for getting on to the bus and rear door for getting off from the bus. Unlike Sitamarhi where bus conductors used to make sure that there is no space left even for breathing, that conductor of DTC bus did not give a shit about the number of passengers and asked the driver to start the bus. I was surprised.

The roads were well maintained and wide enough to accommodate three buses side by side on a single lane. It was simply amazing for me. Though I had been to Delhi during summer breaks every year yet I did not notice all that before. I was too small and innocent to discover those differences between Sitamarhi and Delhi then. All I used to have in my mind was to have as much fun as I could have at maternal grandma's place. Anyways, the bus kept on moving swiftly and I looked if they too had installed a TV to play movies. Papa laughed and told me that there was no such thing in any of those buses in Delhi. I was slightly disappointed. I asked for his mobile phone. I played

Tetris, a tile matching game on that Motorola cell phone. That game seemed addictive to me as it was the very first time I was operating a mobile phone. I did not realise how time flew on that bus. After one hour of smooth bus ride, we got off at a stop which read 'Sagarpur'. I had never heard of that place before. The name seemed fancy, though. However, the bus stop was very dirty.

There was a stack of garbage in a pyramid shape just beside the stop. About 50 people including elderly, women, men, boys and teenage girls were waiting for their respective buses. Some were sitting, some standing while some were busy with their mobile phones. Some trolleys were selling water, cigarettes, cucumbers and other tobacco products. Some portable stalls were preparing fast food items such as burgers, Chow-Mein and samosas. Huge line-ups of people purchasing tokens so as to grab their plate of Chow-Mein took me by surprise. I asked papa about how much time it would take us to reach home. He told me that we were almost there. All we had to do was walk for five minutes. We crossed the road and entered into a street filled with people roaming here and there as if they had no idea where to go. The street was very narrow and had houses on both of its sides. We then took right turn and entered one of the streets which was even narrower, walked about 50 metres and took another turn into another street, entered another street after that street, took left and there came another street besides a street, we skipped that street and entered another street towards right of that street we had skipped and finally, entered a street with no street ahead. It was a long one-way street! I could see that there are no further streets after that one.

'Shukar Hai!' (Thank you, almighty!) I chanted inside my mind. Papa kept on walking and I was following him. Meanwhile, I was thinking of that area where we had rented a small floor. 'Am I really in Delhi, what kind of place is this? It is

too congested! What kind of people I saw on my way! Is this going to be our home for next couple of years?' these were some of the haunting questions which came into my mind. It was an 'urban-slum', I must say. I kept mum and was guessing about our home. I pointed out several houses and asked papa couple of times whether I guessed it right or wrong. I was wrong all the times. Seconds before that never Ending Street was about to come to an end papa opened the gate of the second last house built on the right side of that street. Oh lord! I heaved a relieving breath. But 'Wait! Let me hold Angel for you', papa said. 'Now what the hell is Angel' I thought inside my mind. But 'Who Angel?' I asked politely. Even before papa could answer my question I heard a bark and I was like 'oh shit!' They had a dog. It was continuously barking and soon started running downstairs towards me. I was more irritated than I was horrified to see that dog running towards myself. Despite being so close to animals in Sitamarhi, I never liked or wanted to have one around me every time. It was a small female dog covered in white fur. I had not much knowledge about dogs yet I guessed it was a Pomeranian. That bitch came closer to me and started smelling my shoes and legs. Papa held its belt and told me to climb upstairs. I did so. By then the frequency of that bitch's bark was significantly decreased.

I reached the first floor and was about to take a turn on the platform so as to climb upstairs for the second floor where we lived. Right then, I saw a girl standing in front of a mirror and washing her face religiously in the wash basin. She had applied some sort of brown sticky paste on her face. I could not see her face properly as I climbed quickly upwards. Although, I had a glimpse of her in that fraction of second. While stepping upwards, I thought she might be that girl, Leema who used to pick my call every time I called Delhi from Sitamarhi. I reached the second floor and could see brother sitting in his room watching TV. He saw me and shouted 'Mommy! Bhaiya (brother) is here!' He then opened the door for me. Mommy came as soon as I entered, I touched her feet and sought blessings. Mommy and brother were very excited to see me and so was I to meet them finally. I asked in excitement about where everybody else was. I got to know that chachu had gone to work and chachi had gone to her parents' home. I also got to know that she was about to give birth to a baby soon. That was a good news. Then I confirmed with mommy if that girl was Leema or not. I was right, she was Leema.

I noticed we had a room cooler in our home. Room coolers were something I had never seen in any of the houses in Sitamarhi. We did not need to have one there as summers in Sitamarhi were much relieving than that in Delhi. Delhi is hot as hell in summers. I changed my clothes and asked mommy what she had made for dinner. It was my favourite Paneer (Indian cottage cheese) that night. Mommy made it purposely as she knew I would love to eat that for dinner.

I waited for chachu to come. He came at around seven in the evening. I met him and showed him those 50 rupees which he gave me when he left Sitamarhi. He was surprised to see that I never spent that money. Anyways, we had our dinner together. After that, I showed my transcripts and other documents to everybody. We also made a phone call to Shankar and told him to call grandma and grandpa to his booth. After few minutes we called him again and grandma was on the phone line. I talked to her and told her about my time spent in Chandigarh and my journey to Delhi. I got to know that grandpa had not returned from the shop till then. Grandma had a word with papa and suggested him to come to Sitamarhi as they had arranged for a buyer. After talking on the phone we all went to bed. Well, there was no bed though, we had to sleep on mattresses lying on the floor. But who cares. One thing that was amazing was electricity supply in Sagarpur. The moment I thought 'Waow! At least we have electricity here.' Poof! It was gone. Fan and cooler stopped and I felt the heat of Delhi's summer. Anyhow, I fell asleep.

12

Welcome to Life!

Next morning, I wanted to sleep for some more time but the continuous harsh and loud shout of 'sabzi-wala' (vegetable seller) compelled me to wake up. I did not get up even then. Seconds after, I heard the even louder voice of 'kooda-wala' (garbage collector) guy. Now, they both were shouting to their maximum capacity. The street was one side open and narrow so their sound was echoing and seemed amplified. I could not tolerate that shit and woke up with an annoying mood. Brother wished me 'Good Morning!' 'Good Morning, indeed!' I replied sarcastically. He laughed at my helplessness and I sat there looking at him. I saw mommy quickly going downstairs to buy some vegetables. I asked brother where papa and chachu were. He told me they would leave for their respective jobs at 6.45 in the morning, every day except Sundays.

I stood in the balcony and peeped down to have a look what was happening in the street. The moment I stood there I saw people from houses to my right, left and front were already on their balcony's and they stared at me all at once as if I was from Jupiter. Their interrogative expression was asking me 'who the hell are you?' repeatedly. I did not give a damn, though. I saw women of the entire street gathered there to either buy some veggies or to throw their garbage in that koodawala's big trolley or to do both. Most of them were almost quarrelling with that veggie guy to lower the prices. There were some small kids shouting and playing cricket. I could feel depressed. Meanwhile, I saw one girl coming out of the house built right in front of my house. She looked above (as if she knew I was looking down into the street) and saw me. We had an eye contact for few seconds. She seemed elder than me. Seconds after, I saw Leema leaning with the railings of her balcony below me. She was picking her nose, with great focus and dedication. We all pick our nose some time or the other, but seeing someone picking their nose is yuck! I just could not handle that and came back to my room. Depression confirmed!

Mommy returned somehow considerably late and had some polybags full of different vegetables in her hands. I asked her where she was. She then told me that almost everyone in the neighbourhood was asking her about me. So she had to tell everybody that I am her elder son, who came from Sitamarhi and will stay with them from now onwards.

Midst all these instances I discovered people, especially women really don't mind their own business. They have to have all the information of what's happening around them even if it is of no use to them. Mommy asked me to get fresh and come for breakfast. I felt nature's call coming to me and stood up to it but found that brother was taking a shower. We had only one bathroom which had attached toilet. I 'ordered' him to come out right there right then. Even after knowing the torture I was going through, he instead neglected and laughed crazily from inside. I knew I was not in a position to argue or to bargain with him. Therefore, I 'requested' him gently and finally he came out.

Now the even bigger problem was standing, rather sitting before me. We had western style toilet in our rented home.

I used Indian style toilet for my entire life in Sitamarhi. Since my birth, I had never come across Western style toilet. There was a war going inside my mind or to be specific, inside my stomach. It seemed as if the whole world was standing against me. What could I have done then? I just appreciated human nature and accepted whatever the hell situation offered me. My journey to a wonderful world of sufferance and tyranny had just begun. That paneer I had eaten last night did 'Phhrrrt... Brrrt...KRRAK THOOM!' 'Welcome to life! Gaurav', I sarcastically complimented myself in my mind. 'Phhhrrt, Fart'.

13

THE CONCEPT OF JUGAAD

One of the biggest concerns for me apart from adapting to Delhi's culture and the environment was to get admission in any of the schools in grade tenth. I did not want to waste my time and sit at home doing nothing but tolerating my neighbourhood for one year.

There was a protocol in Indian education system those days. Students had to complete their grade ninth and tenth from the same school as the registrations for CBSE grade tenth board exams were done in grade ninth only. Also, they had to pursue grade eleventh and twelfth from the same school as well, because registrations for grade twelfth boards would get done in eleventh grade. This became a serious problem for me. Either I had to get my admission in grade ninth again or else I had to do some work-around to seek for a 'jugaad' (hack). I chose the latter. I simply did not want to get admission in ninth grade for the second time.

I spoke to papa and chachu regarding that. They further spoke to some of their known but nothing worked out. It was not an easy task to do. Moreover, no school would agree on accepting me directly in grade tenth. We did not know anyone in the education sector in Delhi. Had someone came to Sitamarhi for admission, grandpa would just have made a simple phone call and everything would have been right on track. But things were not that simple this time. I tried applying in many schools, both online and in-person but every school rejected my application. Soon, summer vacations were about to begin. Schools in Delhi would be closed for two months and reopen in the month of July. I tried my best but I failed every time.

In a blink of an eye, the month of May arrived. Schools were closed for two months and I had no option but to wait until their reopening in July. I was more stressed than ever. I had started to believe that I had lost both the option. Neither I would get admission in grade tenth and since it was too late in July to ask for admissions, nor I would get admission in ninth grade. Therefore, I would have to wait for one year and then take admission in ninth grade. Oh shit! It would take two more years to get into grade tenth. I was worried, too much worried. My family could see that tension on my face, everyday.

Mommy had her elder sister who lived in Rohini, one of the biggest sub-cities in Delhi. I suggested her to talk to her sister and see if she or anyone in her family could do something. Mommy made the call and told her sister about my concern. Masi (mother's sister) then asked her father-in-law if he knew someone who could get me into grade tenth in any school. Luckily, he responded in affirmative. He had lived there since ages and therefore, had some solid contacts.

Things in India work that way sometimes. When everything fails, jugaad works! It felt as if I had almost won a lottery. A ray of hope emerged out of nowhere. Without further due, we decided to visit Masi's home next day. I was feeling happy that day. Next day, I and mommy visited Masi's home in Rohini. Soon Masi's father-in-law took me along with him to their friend's home. Upon reaching there, I got to know that elderly person himself was the Principal of a government school in sector 6 of Rohini. He listened to me and understood my situation. After thinking for few minutes he asked me if I could take an admission test so as to get admitted in his school. I could do almost anything to get my admissions. An admission test seemed nothing to me, I just said yes instantly.

He then called us to his school next day. I was a bit nervous that time. 'What if I fail this test?' What would people think of me upon failing this test?' these were few questions in my mind. Anyways, next day we visited his school. By that time, I had memorised the entire way of reaching that school from Masi's house. Principal Uncle gave me a question paper which had a mixture of English grammar questions, mathematical problems, and some essay type questions. The test appeared to be very easy. After I began doing it, I realised it was actually very easy. 'What's the point of giving such a test to me?' I wondered while doing my exam. After about half an hour I was done with the test.

Meanwhile, Principal Uncle and Masi's father-in-law were having tea and cookies and were laughing like anything. Since summer break was on and nobody was there in the school except some clerical staff, I decided to take a look at that school. I asked Principal Uncle about it and he encouraged me to roam around. I took a round and found it was nowhere similar to the schools I had previously been to. Infrastructure was devastating, classrooms were very dirty, light bulbs were homes to spiders and insects, benches were broken and windows and switch boards were malfunctioned. The only thing appeared to be fine in most of the rooms was blackboard. It seemed black; and fine too. Several classrooms had their walls painted with sprays. Some had scratches on them, seemed as if students intentionally scratched them. It was too much for me to digest when I saw one of the rooms graffiti-fied with 'fuck', 'asshole' and '*bhencho*' written on one of its walls. When I looked outside the room, it said 'Grade 5, Section B'. Kids were growing fast. I knew where my fate was taking me in future. I had no choice left.

With a heavy heart, I returned to the office. I saw some empty glasses which had cold drinks in them when I had left, some plates with two or three cookies left and few cups of tea. I thought of informing Principal uncle about what I had just seen. But then I thought what do I say to him? I mean it does not seem right to say 'Sir, there is fuck, asshole and *bhencho* written all over the wall.' I could not figure out a decent way to say that and had to resist myself and let go. After all, I was not going to stay there forever, right? Who knew!

Anyways, by that time Principal Uncle had checked my test and informed me that I am eligible to be admitted. *'Beta aap (dakaar) pass ho (dakaar) gaye',* (Son, you (burp) passed (burp) the test). I was in absolute delight after hearing that burp(y) statement. After some paperwork, I was declared officially in. We came back to Masi's home. I gave that good news to everybody. Everyone was happy to hear that. Mommy thanked Masi's father-in-law and we left for our home. I shall be grateful to their family for this help.

14

GUESS WHAT?

I asked mommy about how would I commute daily from Sagarpur to Rohini and back. It was about one-hour journey in auto-rickshaw, I observed when we were going to Rohini from our home. Mommy decided to show me the bus route as I could not go to school daily on auto-rickshaw. It would be expensive. So we stood at a bus stop nearby Masi's home and waited for the bus number 879. A few minutes later a blue line (Delhi had DTC and private buses which were known as the blue line) bus arrived and we got inside it. There was no rush inside that bus. As soon as we sat the conductor (seemed to be a Haryanvi guy) came and gave our ticket.

Like every other bus conductor, he too had tucked a pen on his right ear. It was a kind of signature style for conductors in Delhi then. If you are a bus conductor, it's fucking important to have a pen tucked, not in your pocket but on the ear or else you will not be deemed as a professional bus conductor. Work ethics, you see! After a little more than an hour, we reached Sagarpur. It was the same bus stop where I had got off while coming from Railway Station.

Nothing was changed as there were about 50 people waiting for their respective buses. Some trolleys were selling water, cucumber and all that smoky tobacco shit. We crossed the road and entered the same street that I and papa entered a few days ago. I knew what was about to happen. A confusing maze of streets and turns baffled my head. I kept following mommy and reached home. I opened the gate and climbed upstairs. Angel did not bark at me that time. I was surprised. While climbing further to my floor I heard a voice calling my nick name 'Shanu'. I turned back immediately and saw Mary Aunty, Leema's mother (and our landlady) standing beside me. 'Namaste Aunty' I greeted her. She nodded. 'Did you get admission?' she asked. I was wondering how she got to know about what I had gone for. 'Yes Aunty, I got admission in tenth grade in a government school in Rohini' I replied. She seemed equally surprised and happy as I was to know that. I kept on climbing the stairs and 'Congratulations! Bhaiya (brother)', I heard another voice. It was Leema standing on the platform and smiling at me. 'What the hell…? what did she just say to me!?' I thought in almost a state of trauma. This was the very first time we both had a face to face communication and I realised not having communication at all felt way better than hearing Bhaiya from her. I was young, I was volatile, I felt like burning her alive.

'Shit…I mean…Thanks, thank you!' I replied confusingly and kept on climbing until I reached my floor. Brother was home and he opened the gate and simultaneously asked if I got admission or not.

'Guess what?' I pretended to be sad.

'What?' he nodded as if he already presumed I did not get the admission. We both were silent for few seconds.

'I fuckin nailed it!! I got admission in tenth!' I shouted in excitement. We hugged each other. Brother was very happy for me but then *'Chal pani la'* (bring some water), I ordered him and his happy face instantly turned into that of an ugly toad. Soon after drinking water I phoned my grandparents in

Sitamarhi and gave them this good news. There was a wave of happiness in my family in both the cities. In the evening, Brother and I went to play badminton in the street. A few minutes later, other kids and boys and girls of my age gathered around us. My brother knew every single one of them and vice versa. Before I could figure out my escape from that street my brother started introducing me to all of them. I had no other option left but to shake hands with them and pass a fake smile as if meeting with them was the most fabulous moment of my life in Delhi.

As I was about to enter my house I saw that same girl who looked up and saw me staring down into the street another day. One of the girls whom I had just shook hands with shouted 'Roopa…meet him, he is Shanu, Aman's brother.' And I got to know her name was Roopa. We both shook hands and I smiled…well, this time genuinely! She looked way better than other girls I saw in my *mohalla* that day. Since Roopa had a fair complexion and glowing skin I presumed she must be highly educated. I was a kid back then and would often judge people's qualification by their looks.

Right after that, I rushed inside my house. While climbing up I saw Leema cleaning her face with some kind of herbal paste; it seemed green so I thought it must be herbal. She quickly went inside so as to keep me from seeing her in that condition. 'Huh! Poor girl trying to improve skin tone of her face.' I offered my sympathy to her in my mind while nodding my head sideways. I took a shower as I was sweating profusely after playing badminton. I slept early that night. After about two hours or so mommy woke me up forcefully and ordered me to eat my dinner. I was tired as fuck and could not even open my eyes fully. But mommy did not care, all she wanted was to make me eat my dinner. I had never skipped my dinner. I would be okay if I don't eat anything in daytime, but I had to have my dinner or else I could not sleep, neither I would let anybody sleep.

15

GET ME OUT OF HERE!

It seemed as if the month of July arrived pretty soon that year. Well…that month was about to change my life, forever. I had my school starting in the first week of July. No one in my family had an iota of what my school was like. They were happy for me.

Now, I was even more tensed than I was earlier. I realised not getting admission in any school felt better than thinking about going to that government school. In a blink of an eye, the judgement day arrived. Mommy's cell phone rang loudly and completely woke everybody else in my family except me. I was half asleep even then. Something was there in the background of my subconscious mind. I felt a fear that reminded me of going to school. I opened my eyes and left my bed with lightning fast speed.

It was 4.30 AM in the morning. Fucking 4.30 AM! Who wakes up that early in the morning to go to school? But I had to, as waking up at 4.30 AM would allow me to leave for school by 5.15 AM. Then, I had to catch that bus number 879 which would drop me to Sector 6 bus stop in Rohini by 6.30 AM. Also, I had to keep some buffer time for walking backwards in case I fall asleep on the bus and miss my bus stop in Rohini. Then I was supposed to take a 15-minute walk from there to my school. Hell of a schedule that was! I had told mommy not to wake up that early for me to prepare my breakfast and lunch. Instead, I preferred getting some pocket money for spending on my meal which I was supposed to buy from the school canteen.

After all that hassle, I finally reached my school. I arrived pretty early that day. It was my first day and I did not want to be late. I noticed the main gate of my school was still locked. There was no sign of the man. However, two stray dogs, a pile of tree leaves, scattered garbage and lots of mosquitoes were there to accompany me. 'Welcome to this Sarkari (government) School, Gaurav.' I thought with a heavy breath. After sitting on a plank nearby school gate for 15 minutes, I saw one thin tall man coming towards the gate. It was clear that he was appointed as night-guard of the school. However, he used to spend away his nights in deep slumbers. What took me by surprise was not his carelessness towards his duty. It was his uniform/attire on duty. He was wearing an underwear and a torn vest which said *'yeh aram ka maamla hai.'* He implemented that statement literally in his life, I could see that.

Anyways, he stared at me while opening the gate as if I had committed a serious crime by arriving that early. Probably he too was equally shocked to see me there as I guessed he must have never seen any student coming so early to school. He directed me to enter the premises. I nodded and entered. The place was not new to me as I had seen every nook and corner of that school. I walked towards my classroom which was right next to the boy's toilet. I inhaled a devastating smelly air while crossing the toilet door. 'Yuckk, get me out of here!' this came out of my mouth.

I grabbed the very last seat in class as I did not want anybody to notice me at the very moment they enter the classroom.

I was very shy and reserved. Soon I could hear footsteps of children going for their respective classes and then, more intense footsteps. I was excited and nervous at the same time. I was about to stand up and take a look outside but then a girl entered my class and all my courage disappeared. She smiled at me and asked if I was newly admitted. I got to know that she too was new in the class. The moment I was about to feel comfortable I witnessed an exodus of students entering my class. Some of them were shouting and swearing in a friendly manner, some of them were eating, few girls were laughing like witches and few students were still sleeping. I don't know how did they manage to come to school in that condition. Since the room was full of students it started getting hot in there. Fans were running at snail's pace. All I could do was clean my forehead with a handkerchief every now and then.

I was introduced to the entire class by my class teacher and every subject teacher started recognising me. I was good at studies so it was not hard for me to score good marks in tests. This made me friends with some of the toppers in my class. I realised that my class had mixed crown from all over India. Though they were not as decent and sophisticated as students in private or convent schools yet, they were good at heart.

Days turned into weeks and weeks into months. I would always catch the same blue line bus while going to and coming back from school. Somehow the bus schedule matched with my timings. After about a month I became friends with the bus conductor, another Haryanvi guy with a pen tucked on his right ear! Now I would pay only five rupees instead of ten for my ticket to school and five rupees while coming back. That way I started saving ten rupees on a daily basis. It was quite an amount those days for me. I did not tell anybody in my family about this ticket thing. I thought I would lose those ten rupees if I told them about this thing. I did not want to lose that money as

I could eat or do anything with those extra ten rupees without being caught. I was naïve.

The year 2006 had come to an end and I was about to appear in my board exams in next three months. The school was just a formality. Well…it was just for the heck of it from the very beginning. In a 45-minute period, teachers would come 15 minutes late, blabber something for 15 minutes and leave 15 minutes early. Students would stand up when a teacher enters, they would then sleep during the entire class and then half of them would stand up when the teacher leaves. Remaining would still be in deep slumber. Some could manage to eat their lunch in the middle of a class.

Internal tests were more of a circus. Nobody would care if students are cheating or even talking to each other during an exam. Some fellow classmates were a pro in cheating. They would bring the entire fucking course-book into examination hall and then copy answers from it. Hats off! to them. I had never imagined something like that before. I would often feel giving those guys a standing ovation for their fearless attitude in life. This is how things used to be in a 'Sarkari' school in those times. It was that school which showed me that girls can be at par and even ahead of the boys for girls in my class would hide notes, notebooks and even course-books into their uniforms.

Anyhow, I was about to appear in my tenth board exams in March 2007. Few days were left for me to prepare for the exams. There used to be a hype created by parents, teachers and everyone else about board exams. It would project board exams as the iron gate of life. I did not give a damn and took those exams as normal ones. And I nailed it! results were out in the end of May and I secured above 80%. Everybody in my family, school and even *mohalla* was happy for me. Roopa was happy for me and I was happy to see her happy. We both became good friends by then. Lukose Uncle (landlord) and Mary Aunty congratulated me. Leema was happy for me but her ego did not let her personally congratulate me. We had developed a cold war situation between us. And I thought I fucking cracked that so called iron gate of life. Little did I know that a bigger problem was waiting for me beyond that gate...poor me!

16

The Chits of My Fate

After I passed tenth grade, I quit my school. Now I was eligible to get admission in any school and pursue eleventh and twelfth grade from that very school. But that was not the problem as I could get admission very easily in any of the schools in Delhi.

What started bothering me was the stream to be chosen in eleventh grade. Science, commerce and arts were revolving around my head day and night. I had no aim or career objective aligned in my life. I could be a doctor, I could be an engineer, lawyer, pilot, teacher, businessman, even an author or anything that would make me rich, filthy rich. I just wanted to earn money so that my family does not have to see price tags before buying things, they don't have to look for cheaper options available in the market.

I never gave a dusty fuck to what future would bring to me. No one in my family could suggest what was good for me as even they did not have any idea of what I was planning to do in future. I was really confused and tensed. With no clue left, I asked mommy to prepare three paper chits for me. Each stating science, commerce and arts on them respectively. Mommy raised one of her eyebrows and stared at me. She did not say anything but I could figure out her saying 'are you crazy' to me in her mind. To earn majority and add some strength to my stupid decision I phoned grandma in Sitamarhi and told everything to her. Even grandma disapproved my idea of leaving my fate with those chits. I remember her saying *'aa ki gal kitti tu!'* (what is this nonsense!) in Punjabi.

Anyways, there was no option left and I insisted on that lucky draw thing. Brother was excited and started preparing chits for me. Siblings often create trust issues in your life. Same was the case with me. I could see that itch in his eyes while writing on those chits as if he did not care about what I was about to choose. He just wanted to see me go by that funny idea. I finally picked one of them and it said 'science' spelled wrong as 'Siense'. Well…I told you my brother didn't care at all.

Now that it was decided what I was about to pursue I felt a big relief. I had to look for a school to get admission into. I searched the internet, asked my friends and visited many schools nearby. Some were good but were very expensive to study into, some were even better but located very far from my home whereas some schools were really close to my home and were in my budget but low in standard and reputation. Clueless, again! Life in Bihar was way better than that in Delhi, I swear. After a long detailed discussion with my family members, it was decided that I should go to those schools which were good and well reputed regardless of their tuition fee and distance from my home. Family always decides better for you. But I had to interfere, always. I did not want to go far from my home as I knew how difficult it was to commute on a daily basis, that too in a bus! Also, I did not want my family to spend more than necessary on my studies just because I would get an air-conditioned classroom and sophisticated classmates to interact with. Hence, I decided to get into another government school which was located in Janakpuri at five-minutes walking distance from my house.

Nobody in my family had any problem with that as I had already demonstrated good academic result while studying in a government school. Moreover, it was dirt cheap to pay tuition fee there. I had witnessed thunders in my previous 'sarkari' school. But I survived that one year somehow. Getting adjusted to another government school seemed peanuts for me. Well…how could I have foreseen what was coming in my way.

Next week I gathered all my academic and personal documents required to get admission in that government school and rushed. As soon as I made my final turn that was supposed to take me to the school, I saw people along with their children standing in a zig-zag line. They were eating, blabbering, shouting on the road. Some of them were sitting on the road. Almost every one of them had a dark skin tone and hence, I concluded they were poor and illiterate. Did I use to judge people by their skin colour, remember?

'Hmm…there must be some food or cloth distribution ahead.' I thought confidently. A few seconds later it took me by shock to see that line emerging out of the main gate of the same school in which I was going to take admission. *'Oo..bhen…cho…?'* I was stunned. The moment I tried to figure out the way to skip the line and enter the premises, people standing behind me started shouting. They were yelling at me as they thought I was trying to enter the school without being in line. They were absolutely right! I replied back and made them understand I was just seeing what was going on.

'Be in line and then see what's going on!' a fat lady shouted at me. 'Hell yeah! you greasy piece of flesh.' I cursed her in my mind. But 'Yes I am going back in line!' I shouted at her. After standing there for three hours directly under the summer sun of Delhi, I felt like a tandoori naan dipped in butter. I was sweating profusely, I was inhaling bad body odour of others,

I was being pushed ahead, people were stepping on my feet, and I was tolerating all that shit to get admission in a fucking 'sarkari' school that had cracked walls and uncovered sewer nearby.

As soon as I entered the gate I saw a big board saying 'Govt. Boys' Senior Secondary School.' Another wave of shit had stuck on my face. The school was only for boys and it operated from 1 PM to 6 PM. What could I do then, I had to bear it. I entered principal's office and what I saw was not very different from what I had seen in the principal's office of my school in Rohini.

Some glasses which had cold drinks in them, some plates with two or three cookies left and few cups of tea. 'Hell no!' I thought in disappointment. It was pretty big office with some clerks doing paper works, some were interviewing students. The principal did not ask me to sit down. I showed him all my documents and mark sheet of my tenth exam. 'Hmm…good' he said to me. And I thought I nailed it once again, I was wrong again. 'Since you scored decent marks, we insist you take commerce.' The principal said in commanding voice. 'No! I want to pursue science stream.' I was adamant. I saw all of the clerical staff laughing on my decision of taking science.

Something was going on, I could not understand what. Then principal pointed his finger towards a boy who was being interviewed for admission in science stream in eleventh grade. He was not even able to spell simple English words like committee, champagne, psychiatrist and so on. Upon asking about the capital of India, that fellow replied with 'rupee' in his answer. Well, that was smart, I would say. But that clerk rejected his application. I was still assertive on getting admission in science stream. After all, it was decided in the lucky draw. After a short and easy question answer round I was officially admitted to that school. I thanked them and rushed towards my home. That school was going to be in my life for two years.

17

DOOMSDAY

I began going to that school in the month of July. As I was familiar with how things used to work in a government school, I thought it would be pretty easy for me to get along with the crowd of that school. But things were completely different in that school.

Since it was not a co-ed school and operated in the afternoon shift, it had all male teachers! It was even worse than my previous school in Rohini, I soon discovered. Here, teachers seldom came to take the class. Students would often spend their time playing, fighting and eating blackberries after climbing up on trees planted on school's property. If caught by anyone from the school administration, all they had to do was to offer some of their blackberries to the person that had caught them and all was set.

Remember, what I found written in one of the classrooms in my school in Rohini? Well…here kids were one step ahead. They had not only written things on walls, they had shown things with the help of labelled diagrams and sketches. I was doomed. I had only 12 students in my class for those two years. Students would not remember each other's real name as they would call each other by using profane words in a friendly casual manner. I tried my best to keep myself away from any evil. Despite trying my best, I was influenced by my company in school. After spending little more than a year in that school I began turning into one of them. I would not tuck my shirt; I would go to school wearing *'chappals'* and most importantly, I started giving zero fuck to studies. The school was just a time pass by then. Soon the day arrived which made me deeply regret my decision of taking admission into that school.

'Beep beep…beep beep' cell phone rang with a lousy tone. Oh lord! Why this phone has to ring everyday so early in the morning, I thought with a very annoying mood. I searched my phone near my pillow and hit the snooze button that too with my eyes closed. It was my daily alarm which was trying to wake me up but was suppressed by me as usual. Meanwhile, grandma also tried to wake me up. She and grandpa had made their permanent move to Delhi from Sitamarhi. We had sold our shop and house. Now my entire family was with me in Delhi.

'Beep Beep…Beep Beep' cell phone rang again, but this time, the ringtone was different from the earlier one. Actually, it wasn't the alarm, but a phone call. 'Now, what!! Who the hell is calling me' I muttered while searching the phone. Soon after grabbing it from the corner of my bed I saw it with only one of my eyes opened. I figured out that it was a call from an unknown but local landline number. I picked up; "Hello!" I said with a heavy and sleepy voice. *"Uth ja bhai, Board ka result aa gaya!!"* (wake up brother, board results are out!!) said the other person on the line. Poof…!! I forgot to breathe for a moment. Before I could understand anything, the phone line disconnected. My senses became attentive and all my sleep vanished after hearing that news. *'Ooo…bhencho…'* With that shocking sensation in my entire body, I woke up rapidly and left the bed…

It was 21st May 2010. The clock showed 10:15 AM and the day was Friday. Doomsday had arrived! I clearly remember that thrill and fear which was continuously popping out of my mind like hell, until I saw my result window on the computer. I took an easy breath and paid my heartiest regards to the mighty self. Yes, I was declared pass. Though I hardly managed to secure 62% in aggregate, still I was at ease as I met all the required criteria for appearing in engineering entrance examinations.

While returning home, I saw a local boy on the other side of the road, who was a bit familiar to me. Though he was an ass I would dearly love to kick, yet I used to pass a fake smile upon seeing him. You know for formality purposes and all that...I was wishing to pass by him without getting noticed. I kept on walking with my fingers crossed and then, "Hey dude...how much you got?" he shouted at me. 'Why me all the time!!' I thought annoyingly. I turned back, waved and said "Bro 62%" with that fake smile on my face. "Could have done better, huh" he replied as if he topped the boards. I did not consider it essential to reply further. I smiled again and moved ahead. "Fuck off! you son of a bitch" I replied him. But this time, inside my mind to avoid any small scale street level world war!!

That year, I tried my luck in almost every National and State level engineering entrance exam but didn't get success. Ultimately, I was left with two options; either to get myself enrolled directly in any of the private colleges across the country or to dedicate one whole good year to prepare for next year's entrance tests. After thinking many times and critically analysing the situation and their circumstances, I chose the latter.

Patience is a virtue after all. I believed in that and decided to take a break from my studies for a year so as to gear up myself for the preparation of the entrance tests which were to be held next year i.e., in 2011. With a hope in my heart that one day I will become worlds' finest computer engineer; I joined a coaching class nearby. I gathered all my concentration and enthusiasm and devoted it to the most messed up combination of subjects in this world i.e. Physics, Chemistry and last but certainly not the least, Mathematics!! Initially, it was alright with me to study these subjects daily for at least two hours each. But after two months it started irritating me. I used to think in every class that why am I studying this crap. What Physics and Chemistry has to do with computer engineering!! And that doesn't mean that Mathematics is tolerable. It was the biggest pain in the ass to me among all the subjects. I somehow managed to keep my frustration and anger under control.

Gradually, in some way or the other, I was getting pissed off from this hectic curriculum. Coaching classes became an unbearable mental torture to me and my batch mates were no less than those patients in a mental asylum. That hope and ambition in my mind of becoming an engineer was the only string that kept me on my track and boosted me to go through all that stuff. Well, days kept on passing and became weeks and weeks turned into months. It felt like the whole world around me was moving forward and progressing and I was still engaged in cleaning up the mess created in my mind by these good for nothing derivations, outdated and pathetic numericals and of course, these chemical reactions of no worth!!

18

What Next?

With all those crest and troughs, one year had gone. Next year, in the month of March, I filled up forms again. That time not too many but only two. But destiny had some different plans for me.

A few days later, my cousin came and boasted a lot about his recruitment as a reporter in a popular news channel of the country. And yes, that was more than enough to confuse an already confused guy about his career. It created a modern day Mahabharata in my mind. To be on safer side, I too filled up the Journalism and Mass Communication entrance form as he did three years ago.

As I was free and had nothing to do as such, I planned a trip to my Bua's place in Dhanbad for a month to enjoy the summers. And I enjoyed it so badly that it made me forgot to take one of the entrance tests I opted for. All my bright summer sunny days turned out into dark nightmares. After realising that I had lost one opportunity with which my career was associated, I started taking life seriously, well till the next sunrise only!! LOL. After spending a month with ease and calm at Sangita Bua's place, I returned to Delhi with a refreshing zeal. It was my second engineering entrance test on next day. I slept little earlier so that next day I could reach on time at the venue. Well after few hours the sun brightened the day and I left for the destination.

Though the day was Sunday, yet there was an exodus at the venue. I got entry at 10 AM sharp. After three hours of extensive mental exercise, I came out with an expression of relief on my face. I roamed across that place for few hours, ate some street food and returned to the home. "Hey, how was your exam buddy?" asked my brother with excitement. "Oo classic it was!!" I replied with a not-so-confident tone. I couldn't give my best but was pretty sure that I will make it this time. Next day it was my Mass Communication entrance test so I went to the bed earlier. That night I couldn't sleep at all. I was continuously talking inside my mind with myself about what to choose as my career, whether engineering or journalism and mass communication? Amidst all this hodgepodge, Leema kept texting me to remind me about her exam. I had to teach her mathematics and science next day as she was about to take her tenth board exams.

'Beep Beep…Beep Beep' cell phone rang and I woke up. After bathing and having my breakfast I left for the venue. My examination centre was in Hameed Pur. It was a place as similar to the hell. No conveyance, no connectivity at all. Somehow I managed to reach there in time. It was cluttered, though, but not as messed up as it was on the previous day. People were reading books and magazines as if what they were reading will surely come in the exam. "Excuse me, what is the time by the way?" a girl standing nearby asked me while pointing her hand to the wrist of her other hand. Before I could answer her, a boy standing near her replied "Its 9:50". And I clearly saw that really big smile on his face as if he had achieved something really important. "Thank you!" said the girl with attitude. Before that boy could utter something really bullshit, the girl moved ahead.

Bell rang and I rushed inside the hall. It was a three hours' objective test. I completed it in time and returned to the home.

"How was it?" asked my brother. "Superb", I replied, but this time with confidence.

After 16 days, both the results came out. I secured rank 13992 in B.Tech and 243 in BJMC. I was eligible to get admission in GGSIPU for both the courses. And again it was a dilemma for me to choose one path.

When life gives you a lemon you make lemonade. But I do not! I throw that lemon at someone. Once again I asked mommy to make chits. This time four of them, two saying BJMC and rest two B.Tech on them. Everyone in my family gathered to see that 'lucky draw', of my life. I closed my eyes and picked one of them. Mommy had already opened remaining three chits even before I could open mine. She was more excited to see what I had got. She shouted 'you have got to do BJMC.' And I was all set to go for it. That is how I take very important decisions in my life! Silly, huh?

Counselling schedules were declared on the university website. I prepared myself and hence my documents required for the counselling. It was July 6, 2011. I went to the counselling venue which was a college nearby my place. As soon as I entered the venue, I saw a very large playground covered up with a bright green carpet of grass. Halogen lights which were fitted on both the sides of the ground were really humongous and were kissing the clouds. Just near that, there was a levelled cricket pitch and a basketball court too. The open air cafeteria was not less than a luxury to me. Well, this was more than enough for me to fall in love with the campus. I optimistically thought that the college which I was going to choose in counselling would also have a radiant environment and huge playgrounds along with a superb canteen. Now who cares about the classrooms and library!! After taking a quick round of the campus, I reached the hall were my counselling was about to start.

I went inside and what I felt was not much different than what anybody would feel inside a circus. Rather a fish market. It was a total chaos. Everybody else was accompanied with their parents, friends, boyfriends and girlfriends, except me. I was all alone yet at my peace. After quickly inspecting the hall with my eyes, I grabbed one seat at the rear of the hall. I prefer sitting at the back because it feels that nobody can watch my back and I can watch everybody's every movement. It gives me a supreme sort of feeling as if I have a command over others. Stupid huh? I know.

After tolerating Delhi's summer sun's torture, tendering yourself freely into the arms of a fluffy chair and that too in an air conditioned hall is no less than eternal bliss! I must say. I was about to sleep in that chair. "Good afternoon, we are about to start the admissions. Please pay attention to your respective rank calling. Thank you." This loud and clear voice penetrated and banged into my head through my ears. Aarrgghh....all my comfort and relaxation flew away. Everyone started arranging their documents as per the serial number mentioned on the board. I took a look into my file folder in which all my documents were kept and it seemed okay to me. Keeping that folder in the chair next to me, I started waiting for my turn to come. I saw my watch, it ticked 2 O'clock sharp.

Meanwhile, a lady along with her daughter (I guessed) crossed my row and while passing by, thrashed my foot with her pin pointed heels. "Oops...Sorry! Did it hurt?" asked the lady with a concerning tone. 'Hell yeah lady!! It did hurt me badly.' I replied her in my mind. But, "Oh no aunty!! It's perfectly alright!" I replied her with a fake smile as if it was really so sweet of her to do so. Anyways, that lady and the girl sat next to me. I saw my watch again and it was 2:05 PM. hardly five minutes were gone and it seemed like I have been waiting since last five hours!! Well, that girl was soon engaged with her paper works but aunty was more interested in my folder. As soon as I took out my rank slip, she popped out to her girl "He has got 243." The girl nodded her head and was still busy in filling up her college preference sheet. Probably she was not much interested in listening to her mom at that point of time. Maybe out of hurry or stress, I guessed. But somehow this ignorant attitude of that girl triggered an uncontrollable urge in my mind to peep into her rank slip now.

'Let me see what she has got now' I thought with a curious sensation. I made few efforts in my own unique weird way and got success. She had slightly better rank than mine. 'Just a little better.... Makes no such big difference....' In this way, I pacified my own emotions.

I somehow managed to see her name and the choice of colleges she mentioned in her preference sheet. Her name was Ishita Arora and she wrote JIMS Vasant Kunj as her first choice among all the colleges to get admitted into. My preference sheet was totally blank. I did not fill it at home as I was not sure about the best college I could get with my rank. Moreover, I had always selected my preferences with the help of chits! But Ishita's decision somewhere left an impact on my mind subconsciously. Now I was a bit inclined towards choosing JIMS Vasant Kunj for me as well.

Meanwhile, a girl with brown skin and curly hairs returned from the counselling desk to her seat. When asked by her friend about the college she got, she happily shouted "Yes!! I got JIMS." The girl was Aanchal. I noticed one of her friend calling her with this name.

Now I was even more confident of choosing JIMS for me; less because I wanted to go for it, more because everybody else wanted to go for it. I made up my mind and was about to fill up my preference sheet but suddenly, "Rank 218, Ashwarya Dubey please report on the dais.... Rank 218." announced the same university representative with a frustrated voice. I halted and my eyes started searching that girl whose name was announced. Within seconds, Dubey stood up, took her documents and stepped out of her row. She was sitting two rows ahead of me. Though I was not able to see her from the front yet she seemed to be pretty. I could figure it out. After dealing with the formalities at the counselling desk, she turned back in a hurry. Maybe she had some other important works to do. She came closer and was clearly visible to me now….and "Waow" I muttered in fascination, my heart skipped a beat and then… *"Oo…kamaal!* You're so beautiful, so damn beautiful… beautiful…beautiful" that was what exactly clinked out of my heart. Yes! This famous track sung by the living blackboard of this planet. It was a visual relief for me to see her. She was an absolute beauty like I have never seen before!! I was amazed and it is almost impossible for me to express that feeling in words. Being in boys' school for two years made me even more sensitive towards beautiful girls. I had not even thought of girls while I was in that school. I just could not control my emotions when I saw her.

Right after Ashwarya left the hall, that announcer called Ishita. The moment she stood up I moved my legs considerably under the chair trying to protect them from being hurt again. Meanwhile, her mother asked about my preference. I simply told her that I too was choosing JIMS. She became even more conscious as her daughter had chosen the same college. I knew what she was thinking. 'Aunty my name is Gaurav. I may look like a labourer, but I am not originally from Bihar.' I said her, in my mind, though. Well, minutes later it was my turn to go to the podium. I proceeded and everything went well. I was admitted in JIMS, Vasant Kunj campus for the morning shift. I came home and told everyone about my admission in the college. Papa brought some sweets so as to celebrate. Finally, a tiring day came to an end.

19

A High School Without Uniform

In the first week of August 2011, I had my orientation in the college. I went along with papa. My college was pretty far from home but well connected with transit. As I entered the gate I saw two guards standing right next to it. They checked my admission form and slips, provided me and papa with an ID card which said 'visitors' and asked us to proceed.

I was happy as they both were in professional uniforms. It somehow reminded me of that day when I saw that *'yeh araam ka maamla hai'* guy. Sigh. Papa asked what had happened? I told him I was recalling my days spent in that government school in Rohini. To cut the conversation short, I simply told him that the college is pretty much same as my school was. Papa had never been to my school. *'Sarkar ka school tha bete. Koi Mazak thodi tha.'* (it was a government school son, not a joke) he said confidently. *'Bilkul theek.'* (rightly said, father) I smiled at his innocence and we entered the building.

I could see the reception from outside the building as well. I showed my enrolment slip to the lady sitting there and she told me to go to T1. 'And where is T1?' I asked her immediately. She gave me a tough look and said 'Tee is the third floor and

1 is room number. So T1.' I was sure she must had answered this question several times before. How the hell would I know that! In my school, T stood for toilet and T1 meant toilet number 1. Anyways we both climbed up to the third floor and could see our room. It was pretty big, had four air-conditioners installed, I could see a projector as well. Moreover, I was happy to see clean walls and a big 'blackboard' which was green in colour. Some students were sitting with their parents. They all had a blank expression on their faces. I imagined how classrooms in government schools were, totally opposite. And I smiled. Papa again asked what had happened. I just nodded sideways.

After ten minutes or so, Ishita entered along with her mom. Soon, Aanchal and Ashwarya arrived. I was now happy from inside to see them in my class. The room was full of students and their parents. There were five chairs and one big long table on the stage. I was wondering who was going to be there for our orientation speech. Moments later, three ladies and two gentlemen came into the room and grabbed their seats.

One of the ladies stood up and introduced herself to us. Her name was Deepa. And she was going to be our class teacher for the entire three year's programme, she told us. Then she introduced other four speakers that I got to know were Director of my college, Head of the communication department, sports journalist and wildlife photographer respectively. Ms Deepa then called upon the head of the communication department, Dr Neeru Johri to address us. It was her first day as well in the college. After her, Dr Ravi Dhar, director of my college spoke. I noticed half of the students and their parents sitting on back benches were sleeping religiously. Ashwarya was looking at her phone, Aanchal was sleeping and Ishita was eating something. Also, there was a boy and a girl sitting just in front of me. They were continuously talking to each other. Seemed as if they knew each other very well. Even if they had known each other, they should have shown some respect to the speakers. *'Saale Bak..cho..d'* (bloody talkative) I supressed my anger. After about an hour, the orientation session came to an end. Ms Deepa requested everyone to gather in T2 to have refreshments. Those who were sleeping on the benches at the back were the first ones to exit from T1 and enter T2. Who doesn't like to have free food? I looked at papa and we decided to leave immediately as it would take us one hour and a half to reach back home by bus. 'How was that?' I asked papa about my college. *'Bahut badhiya.'* (very nice) he replied. He was happy for me.

Next day, I had my classes from 8 AM to 1 PM. I woke up at six in the morning and left home a little early than seven. I reached on time. I was given my college ID card on previous day which I showed to the guards on duty. More and more folks started coming inside the class as it ticked eight in the clock. Soon the room was full and there was a noise created due to their talking with each other all at once. Bell rang and Ms Deepa entered the classroom. Since it was very the first day of the college, she asked all of us to introduce ourselves to the class. I was wondering what to say. Anyways, we all stood up one by one and shared our full name, family background, educational qualification and hobbies.

I remember Ashwarya introducing herself…"Hello! My name is 'Aishwarya.' Aishwarya without an 'I'. I am an army kid. Blah blahblah!" Also, I got to know that my class had four students who had some connection with Bihar. I was feeling relaxed as I knew these people would gel up with me for sure. At least two girls were from the south of India. I could guess as they spelled their names with an extra 'h' in them. They were Krit'h'ika and Nit'h'ya. They both came from the same school and hence were friends with each other for a long time. Some of the girls were from Kashmir (as they claimed). Despite nobody giving damn to them, they used to feel exotic in class.

The majority of my class had Delhi-ites. That day we all repeated same information again and again as every single teacher would ask us to introduce ourselves. The first day of my college came to an end.

I was walking towards my bus stop to catch bus number 604 as soon as possible. I had walked few steps and then I heard someone calling my name from behind. I turned back and saw that same guy who was sitting in front of me on orientation day and was uttering shit from his mouth, nonstop. 'Oh hell!' I muttered. He was having an open bottle of Coca-Cola with him. We shook hands and he told his name 'Ranbijay.' It was now confirmed that he was a Bihari. We shared some of our views about the first day in college until I reached my bus stop.

Next day, I reached college at the same time I had reached previous day. I saw some of the girls and boys from my class smoking behind college premises. There was a 'sutta-point' (colloquial smoking area) at the rear side of my college. And I must tell you, the number of students you will see at sutta point would surpass the number of students you will see in the college at any given point of time. Guaranteed! I could not understand why it was important for some of the students who did not smoke to accompany those who used to smoke.

Anyhow, I entered the class and took my seat at the same place where I was sitting a previous day. Again, Ms Deepa entered the classroom. This time with a book in her hand. She took our attendance and asked all of us to choose four people who would be our Academic Representatives and Class Representatives. I had never heard of these terms. In my school, we had monitors, not AR and CR. Nobody in my class had an idea about whom to vote for the post of AR and CR. It was our second day in the college after all. There was a lot of whispering in the class.

Since we were unable to constitute a common mental conscience, Deepa Ma'am started announcing the names according to her will. She pointed her finger at one of the girls sitting in the very first row of the class. She stood up and told her name to Ma'am. She was Shriya, tall and skinny girl. Then ma'am asked one of those Kashmiri girls to stand up. Her name was Ridhi. After that, she asked Ranbijay to stand up. 'What!? this Bihari is going to be our representative?' I thought in my mind and then 'You! You at the back'. I saw she was pointing in the direction where I was sitting. I was not sure if she was pointing at me or not. I turned back to see who was behind me and saw that clean wall with AC installed on it. 'Oh shit! She is pointing at me.' I was shocked. I had to stand up.

Before I could say anything to her, she said 'Gaurav, you will be the AR of this class.' I wondered how did she remember my name so quickly. 'I am noticing you since past two days. You don't speak at all.' Ma'am added. The moment she said this to me everybody in my class looked back at me, all at once! I felt like a goat in the jungle. My plan was to sit at the back and not to speak much so as to remain low. But my strategy took a dip upside down and resulted in me being highlighted in the class. What could I do then, I nodded in affirmative. Little did I know that it was only me who was going to be assigned to every responsibility and duty of AR and CR. Remaining three were just there for the heck of it.

Few days had gone and I realised almost every fellow classmate of mine seemed to be from rich family. Some had cars, some had motor-bikes, some of them had expensive phones and laptops and some of them would always wear branded clothes. Moreover, they had girlfriends and boyfriends to spend quality time with. Amidst all this, I looked at myself and realised I had nothing, not even a good cell phone. I was nowhere close to them in any aspect.

The amount of money most of them would spend daily on purchasing cigarette surpassed the total cost of my attire, including my undergarments and bag. I was feeling a little out of the place at that moment. I was fearing if I had made the right choice by selecting JIMS as my first preference. It was not easy for someone who had spent previous three years of school life in a government school to settle down among those 'enlightened cosmopolitans.'

My plan of spending three years with those people was simple; I shall not speak at all and sit in the corner of the class room where I could partially hide from the sight of teachers and other students. But everything went wrong. After a while, Ma'am started telling us some rules and regulations to be followed in the college. She began with 'attendance is mandatory, you should not come to college in slippers or sandals, girls should not wear deep neck and mini-skirts, boys must not come wearing pyjamas, nobody will have their phones on the desk' and so on. 'Is this a college or a high school without any uniform?' I wondered.

20

Life in ~~JISM~~ JIMS!

This mischief in the title of this chapter is not an error, its intentional! Searching JIMS on google images would often show results of Bollywood movie Jism back then. Those were the times when ragging was declared an offence by Honourable Supreme Court of India. Prior to that judgement of the court, many students in colleges and universities from all across the county had committed suicide because of being harassed by their seniors in the name of ragging. Luckily, that was not the case in my college. Though some folks from third and fifth semester came to our class in T1 to show their supremacy yet they were unable to do much about that.

However, boys got an opportunity to check out the girls and vice versa. They held a brief introduction round and asked if anyone from my class was interested in entertaining them. My class had a bunch of folks who were dying to show their talent. Some of them sang songs, some of them showed their dance, few were joking around and remaining were enjoying all that. And I was wondering when recess bell would ring and I would go to college canteen to feast upon Chow Mein and burgers. I was a great food-lover back then. It was I who started mixing 'Chat-Masala' in my Chow Mein. Soon, this became a trend among all students as Chow Mein would taste even better with chat masala in it.

A few months later, we all appeared in our final exam for the first semester. I had written my first book on the subject of graphic designing by then. By that time, I knew everyone in my class and everyone started recognising me as well. It was my serious and focused attitude in class that helped me score good marks in final exams. I was declared first in my college. Now, seniors and other teachers would know my name. Even those who were from BBA and BCA programme would know me. Though I treated everyone in my class equally, yet I had become good friends with some of them. Shriya, Sahil, Krithika, Nithya, Deepansha, Ashwarya, Dhun and Ranbijay were closer to me as compared to everybody else. Shriya was a simple and happy go lucky girl. She used to bring tasty lunch for me every day. Perhaps, that was the reason why she was my good friend! Sahil, on the other hand, had a cool personality. He was good looking and would always keep himself well groomed. His photography skills were excellent. Ranbijay and I shared a different Bihari bro-code that was beyond anyone's understanding.

Then there were Ashwarya and Dhun. They both resided nearby my home and Ashwarya would often pick me up in her car for college and drop me while coming from college. In short, that girl for whom I had skipped a beat in counselling session was now my driver! Felt as if I gave life some lemons and it made me a glass of lemonade for myself. Dhun left the college after attending two semesters. She had gone to DU. I barely talk to her on the phone now. However, we had cultivated an understanding between us which shall not let us forget each other.

One of the reasons why I had faith restored in my college was its director, Dr Ravi Kumar Dhar. He used to teach our class in the second semester. He was meditative by temperament and always tried to give more than mere formal education.

His teaching methodology was very simple yet very complex as his command over the English language was phenomenal. I am sure he will score perfectly in IELTS and TOEFL. He had written several academic books and published various research papers. He was working on his debut novel when I was in the third semester. I had written two more books by then. One related to photography in my second semester and another one on development communication. Mr Abhigyan Prakash, a well-known journalist of NDTV had launched my book 'Development and Communication Morphosis' in New Delhi World Book Fair 2014 at Pragati Maidan. My dear friends from NDTV also joined me for the function. I am highly indebted to them.

One more person whom I and Ranbijay cannot forget was our college Registrar, Dr S.K. Dogra. Gosh! That old man was living cannon of JIMS. You are exempt from committing any crime in the college but you dare not do anything stupid that could land you up into his office. Once caught, he would make your college life hell, he was very short tempered. I remember he caught us playing cricket in the college premises. Everybody else ran away and saved their ass but I and Ranbijay stood there and did not notice him running towards us faster than Usain Bolt so as to catch both of us. We both were swearing at each other with great enthusiasm as Ranbijay was not ready to give his bat even after he was declared out. Ranbijay is Bihari by the way.

Anyways, so moments after, we both saw Dogra Sir standing inches away from us. Well...we both still could run away very easily but the professor had seen our faces. We knew that this man would come after us, would find us and kill us eventually. Somewhat similar case as that of Taken, a Hollywood movie. Therefore, we decided to take our chances and stood there as if nothing happened. He quickly grabbed our hands and started dragging us into his office. Seemed as if an old lion was dragging two goats into his den. We had no other choice but to cooperate. As soon as we got inside his office, he started yelling at us with tremendous anger in his eyes. I was about to laugh but somehow controlled it. I realised it could have made the situation even worse. 'By playing cricket inside college premises, you both have taken law in your hands!!' he said in the middle of his entire shouting. Now it was becoming even more difficult for both of us to control our laughter. I mean did we take the law, the 'LAW' in our hands by playing in college? What were they going to do, put a charge on us under Indian Penal Code?!

Things seemed to be settling down after five minutes or so but then I don't know where did he get another impulse of anger from, he grabbed us again and started dragging us to the Director's chamber. Felt as if a butcher was dragging two lambs into the slaughter house. 'Oh no!' I was worried now. I was not afraid of the punishment for our 'crime'. I just did not want Dr Dhar seeing me creating a fuss in the college. I and Dhar Sir shared a different kind of rapport.

Well,...you can face, fight and even win over Dr Dogra but you cannot escape from him. He had to do what he had to do. We both were pushed inside Dr Dhar's chamber. It was my first time I saw his office. Little did I know that his office would become my second classroom in near future. While Dogra sir's chamber was not less than a burning hell, entering Dhar Sir's office soothed all our fear and anxiety. Seemed as if both hell and heaven co-existed in my college without any conflict. Dhar Sir listened to Dr Dogra and requested him to go to his office. The moment Dogra Sir left, Dhar Sir asked us to sit down. We were amazed by his meditative temperament. I and Ranbijay looked at each other and 'Sir *thoda pani milega?'* (Sir, can we have some water?) we both asked at the same time. We were thirsty as we were playing since past two hours. Sir asked one peon to get water for us. Meanwhile, Sir asked us about our studies and whether we have any concerns related to it. 'I don't want both of you to get caught again.' He said calmly. 'Sure Sir!' We both rushed out happily. While crossing Dr Dogra's office we both gave him 'you could not do anything, old man!' kind of look. That was so naïve of us, I now understand.

After few days, we again started playing outdoor games in college. This time, we were even more cautious. Moreover, Dhar Sir had said that he did not want us to get caught again. That meant we were allowed to play without being caught by Dogra Sir. After one more year, my one on one interaction with Dhar Sir became frequent. We would discuss college management, studies, his books, my books, and other important stuff of our lives with each other. During that time, I would often encounter Dogra Sir in his office, Dhar Sir's office or in college premises. We would then have a brief conversation with each other. Eventually, I realised that he was not that 'harsh'. I believe, he too had realised that I was not that of a hooligan. I would often ask him about how was his daughter doing in her studies. He always replied in affirmative. Though I never had any interaction with Deepti in college time, yet I am sure she would do well in her future. After all, she is the daughter of Professor Dogra, the cannon man of JIMS.

One year was gone and college had become my second home. I knew everyone, everybody knew me. We had great interactions with juniors, seniors, staff and teachers. I met some wonderful people who are still connected to me in some way or the other. Well…to maintain the balance of the universe, I came across with some of the morons in my college as well. They were from BJMC, BBA and BCA programme.

I learned something in my college that it is never guaranteed if great minds would think alike; but certainly, it is guaranteed that fools will seldom differ. Though all those stupid people represented different caste, religion, academic fields and sex yet they all were same in their entirety. Time passed by and I was done with my bachelor degree in May 2014. Well…I was, in fact, the top scorer in my college. If you know me and reading this, you probably know I am not joking. Huh?

21

FRIENDS FOR LIFE, AS THEY SAY

I don't know about other things, but I am pretty sure I would always remember my college days until I am dead or affected with dementia. Huge premises, giant infrastructure, sutta point, canteen, library, AC, cooler, fan, T1, T2, T3, attendance, exams, and location of the college…all of that seems next to bullshit in present times. What were you thinking, huh? That I would say something about these things and make you feel nostalgic. Hell no! I've got a life. What's not shitty are the memories, both good and bad, experiences and learnings that I got through friends, foes and teachers in JIMS. It would be unfair on my part if I discuss my college life without disclosing almost everything about those whom I came across in/through college. Yes, almost everything about them!

I remember my very first interaction with Shriya lasted for about 15 seconds or so. Shriya, that tall and skinny girl I mentioned above was an Academic Representative of the class like I was. She came to me one day and asked me to put some designing software in her pen drive. The way she spoke with me was very delicate. *'AAP meri pen drive me wo software daal doge please?'* (Would YOU please put that software in my pen drive?) she said. Who the hell talks like that with their fellow classmates?? In the Hindi language, the word 'aap' is used to mark the respect we have for others especially, elders. 'What the hell did she just speak, AAP!?' I thought in a jolting state. 'Listen, you multi-storey girl, you never say AAP to me!' I blabbered at her. I was upset, I had never received that degree of respect from anybody. So I reacted instead of responding. *'Tu meri pen drive me software daal de.'* (You put that software in my pen drive.), she rectified her previous statement instantly. 'Wow! That was quick!' I thought. This dramatic change in her attitude put Shriya apart from rest of the class, in my mind. Over the course of time, we became friends, after some more time, even better friends. She would always share her lunch with me. We would fight and argue religiously. I enjoyed her company a lot. To be specific, I enjoyed pulling out jokes and passing funny comments on her. My intentions were just to have fun in a friendly manner, yet, there were times when I would often challenge her temperament. She was silly, she was simple and she was innocent. I did not have any problem with her being simple and silly. However, she being too innocent would often create awkward moments among friends. Therefore, I and Sahil decided to drag her out from her innocence zone and make her face the dirty world.

Well...repeating some abusive slangs on a frequent level in her presence, some dirty talks, some 'non-veg.' jokes as they say and few gossips served the purpose. Within six months she had attained the same level of *'chichorapan'* (intensity of being footling) as we did. Now she would not hesitate to express her feelings with a pinch of swearing in it, she was not that innocent anymore. It was for the first time in a very long time that I and Sahil felt honoured; upon making her badass. We accomplished something that day. She lived in Janakpuri, which was not too far from my home. That was one more reason why she and I got along with each other in college really well.

Somewhere in the year 2014, I and Sahil saw Shriya crying at the back of college canteen. Though seeing her crying was not new for us anymore, yet there was something different in her crying that day, we could feel that. Upon asking, she told us about her break-up with her boyfriend whom I and Sahil had once met with. He seemed mentally sound back then. After interrogating a little more, we got to know the reason behind her break-up. 'He does not feel for me anymore. He said he is not interested in me anymore.' Said Shriya while sobbing. 'Bwahahaha, what! haha!' I could not stop myself after hearing that. Sahil was silently watching that weird reaction of mine as instead of pacifying Shriya, I was making fun of her situation. What could I have done then? It seemed funny to me as to how can someone just say two lines and end a relationship that had been in existence from past four years! It's not that I had heard something like that for the first time. But what I had heard before was ending of relationships with a life span of one week, one month or two months' maximum. That's it! For me, it seemed as if girls and boys were changing their monthly calendar or replacing their car engine oil instead of partners. Today with jack, tomorrow with jones. But the situation with Shriya was tragic. 'Everything comes with an expiry.' I thought in my mind. Meanwhile, Sahil was calming her.

Few days after her break-up with that asshole, I asked Shriya about her condition. I wanted to make sure whether she was willing to move on or still could not get her mind away from that. The moment I asked how was everything with her, she started crying like a child. *'Oh bhen..cho!* What did I do?' I was worried. That day, our entire class got to know about her break-up. I guess Deepa Ma'am knew as well. But she could not offer any advice as she herself was lagging behind the scheduled syllabus and needed help with that. Everybody has to deal with their own shit. Few more days had passed, I could not resist myself and finally asked her about how intimate her relationship was. What I got to know was even more surprising than our surprise tests held in college. Shriya told me they both never had a chance to spend some time alone with each other. They never did any adventure together, neither they had travelled places nor they had explored themselves. They never had sex in four years. In fact, they both never kissed each other! 'Then what the hell did you guys do?' I asked in anger. 'Well…we used to talk to each other on the phone, we went on some bike rides nearby my locality, sometimes we used to eat street food together…blah blah!' she was stopped by me in the middle.

'Yaar saath me paapdi-chaat hi khani thi to mujhe le jati. Phone pe baatein to wo apni behen se bhi kar sakta tha. Tune kiya kya hai 4 saal me, mera babu…mera shona!? That's it? Petrol jalaya wo alag. Kuch interesting kiya ho to hi interest aayega na ladke ko! 4 saal se bardasht ki goli de rahi thi tu bas usko. Bechara!' (You could have taken me with yourself to eat street food. He could have talked to his sister on phone. What interesting did you do in those four years? Nothing as such.) And I laughed like anything. After a while, she too got it and laughed crazily. That day onwards, we could see Shriya getting back to normal. Everything was fine in few days after that day. She moved on, I was happy to see her back and so was Sahil. She can thank me later for this!

There were two more friends of mine who resided in Janakpuri and its vicinity respectively. They were Sahil (I mentioned above) and Jaspreet. There is a reason why I mentioned both of them together. I will let you figure that out on your own as Jaspreet is now engaged and hopefully soon be married to same guy she is engaged with. I don't want to take any blames on me.

Anyhow, when it comes to defining a person in one word who has health, looks, skills, courage, attitude and social life along with the latest laptop, car, DSLR and iPhone, Sahil is the answer. Sahil, Jaspreet, Shriya and I would complete the concept of *'Janakpuriya Chhap'* friends. We all would sit together in class and pass funny comments on fellow classmates. In case, we did not find anything to laugh at, Shriya and Jaspreet would be our target. Sahil was a fitness freak back then. Many girls in my class would appreciate his personality as he was good looking and soft spoken. I am not sure if Sahil gave any attention to those girls ever. Well,...he had his social life beyond college as well. Unlike me, who would go directly to my home after college, Sahil liked to roam around and explore different places with his friends. He would often click beautiful pictures with his camera and iPhone. We both had been to Manali together. Despite having differences in our thinking and nature, we both enjoyed that trip. We both talk to each other over facetime at least once every month.

Rare is the combination where beauty meets brains. Ashwarya, my chauffeur and that girl whom I saw in counselling was among those rare combinations. She was not that bright academically. However, making boyfriend(s) at an early age taught her many remarkable lessons in life. After all, no teacher is greater than life itself for life teaches you without any terms and conditions. It was because of her that I began to offend the eyes of some of the morons in my college I discussed before. They would often see her with me and feel jealous. I had no idea about this thing until Ashwarya herself made me realise that. She was enjoying all this, whereas I was concerned. I had never taken her that seriously in my life as it was she who needed my help at each and every step of her college life. It was she who would request me to come to her house and coach her for exams, that too one day before it. It was she who would need my help in persuading her parents over any issue that could lead her into trouble. It was she who would ask for my money in case she fell short of it. It was she who would be always ready to take me to her fashion shoots. She could do almost everything to make me feel okay. Most importantly, it was she who relied heavily on me and trusted me blindly. Now that my college is over, she is being missed badly. I miss those long drives in the car with her through Delhi Cantt. area, I miss her requesting me to help her out, I miss her taking my money for cigarettes and samosas, I miss her asking me to find solutions to every fucking problem of her life. I miss that trust and respect she had for me. She was indeed, my partner in crime. She has a(nother) boyfriend now-a-days in Mumbai. This prohibits me from sharing further about her. By the way, she knows what had happened that day. Ha Ha! She calls me after a certain period of time or whenever she needs any help from me. *'Matlabi hai saali!'* (She is mean!).

If I could go back in time and change one thing about my college life, I would change Dhun's decision of leaving my college and going to IP College for Women. I am being selfish here. She left JIMS after completing the second semester and took admission in IP College so as to pursue a same degree course. She had to do it all over again, her one year spent in JIMS was wasted. I don't know her exact reason behind doing this. I guess she must not be happy with the teaching methodology of our photography teacher. Dhun lived just across the road where I lived. That is why we would often meet with each other coincidently at Sonu Juice Corner, a famous juice shop in Sagarpur. I remember her taking part in a fashion show competition organised by our college. She wore something green and white and looked absolutely stunning. I still have her in some photographs of that fashion show. She was a sport and I owe her a big time for making my college life joyous. I cheer a different level of friendship with her. However, there is something she owes me as well. Dhun, when are you going to return me my Moser-Baer pen drive which you took three years ago?! Probably never, never mind!

I have always liked south Indian cuisine very much. I was a food lover and could do anything to get Idli-Sambhar and Masala Dosa. Talking of Idli-Sambhar always reminds me of Nithya, that girl who puts an unnecessary 'h' in her name. Well…it's her name, her wish. Apart from smoking tens of cigarettes daily, spending more time outside the college premises than inside classroom and wasting time in pubs and clubs with those who were more of a parental liability, Nithya also knew how to deceive our teachers in college. Well…jokes aside. She could never do all this at all. Nithya was one of the most versatile girls I had ever seen. She was declared Miss Fresher after all. She was small in height but had a very big heart. She was short on temperament but had long lasting determination. Despite being so much different from each other, we two used to extract hell lot of fun in each and every class. Though we both put ourselves in danger of being caught, yet my good image would not let teachers doubt on us for creating disturbance in class. Truly said, like poles repel and unlike poles attract each other.

I remember she would often imitate Neeru Ma'am's 'Haina' and instantly I would add 'Montana' to it so as to make it sound like 'Hannah Montana.' And then the entire row would laugh like anything. Crazy we were. We both would go to a famous place nearby our college to eat South Indian food. I would order Idli-Sambhar whereas, Nithya liked to have Parotta Kurma. Krithika and Simran would also accompany us often. Nithya would also bring Idli-Sambhar exclusively for me sometimes. I enjoyed saying no to others upon asking me for sharing that Idli-Sambhar. I cannot thank her enough for making college full of fun. She pursued her masters from Amity University. We are almost out of each other's reach now.

Did you have that one friend who was never serious about his/her career? That one friend who never gave a shit to studies throughout the semester and would go haywire just one night before final exams? Yeah! That erratic one, did you have?

I had one in my class. She was Krithika, a hybrid created when Punjab and Kerala happened. If you know what I mean. I saw her first in the very first week of August 2011. College had just started and we all were settling down into its environment. I had to write everybody's name on a paper as I was assigned to some work of distributing notes among students. I was 'The AR', remember? She came to me and told her name. I wrote her name as 'Kritika' as anybody would write unless there are some conditions applied to it. She took that paper from me and inserted an 'h' between her name. *'Malluu Bhenn..choo!'* I thought in excitement. Meanwhile, I noticed she had a same cell phone as I did. It was Samsung Galaxy Ace. 'Same Same.' I said with a smile. 'Oh yes. Give me your number?' she said. That was for the first time in my life a girl had asked my number that quick. What was the wait then, we exchanged our numbers and soon started chatting with each other on the phone almost every single day. She would always text me 'happy writing' as I was writing my book on Development Communication back then. I was pretty confident that I would pass this course easily and hence I never studied as such. She was pretty sure that I would teach her everything just one night before exams, therefore she never studied as such.

Dude, if you are reading this, which I am sure you are, then do that Anish Sir's 'beta tum fail ho!' stunt. Do it, NOW!

Anyways, as we both knew Punjabi and Malayalam, communication between us had always turned out to be funny and interesting. We have an understanding beyond ordinary between both of us. She texts me sometimes. She has the aim of becoming an IAS officer one day. However, she is working with POPxo and her bio says this "Writer, thinker and a sucker for clothes! Faith keeps me going and I love possibilities!". I hope someone from POPxo does not read this. I told you she was not serious about her career. Thanks, for nothing, though!

After one year had passed in the college, I noticed Krithika roaming around with some other girl quite often. Upon asking, she told me that girl was her school friend and studied in the evening shift of same BJMC batch as ours. That girl was easy, she was uncomplicated. By the way, I am not in talking terms with that girl anymore. However, there used to be a time when she was closest to my heart. She was the one I would spend most of my time with. Her not being very open and social with others made her much like me. Hence, we were able to connect with each other without conflict. There was a time when both of us would be on the phone for hours and hours talking and texting each other. We would talk about college, class, her life, my life, further studies, future, travel, the world, news, anything and everything we wanted to talk about. And now I am finding it hard to initiate any conversation with her. Everything comes with an expiry, I remembered. And no, she was not my girlfriend! In fact, she had never been anyone's girlfriend ever since she broke up with the guy whom she was the girlfriend of, for years.

Everybody in my class had formed their groups as soon as they all knew each other remarkably well. It was obvious and natural for us to find and connect with those who were more or less same as we were as an individual.

The best group of friends in my class had Priya, Swati, Ankisha, Sandeep, Ajay, Sagar, Zishan, Karandeep, Vanshaj, Meghna and Amanpreet, Ridhi, Akhil, along with some less important people like Deepak, Zohaib, Diksha, Rajesh and almost everybody else remaining. I called them less important not because most of them were from Bihar or Haryana, I called them so because they were reserved in nature and would often agree with whatever their group decided for them. I never interacted much with this group. Yet, I would always enjoy being with them whenever and every time I got a chance. I am not in regular touch with them ever since I left college. However, we all are potentially connected via Facebook.

Then there were some, who had their own small world for they did not bother to get along with anybody in my class. They had their own priorities and works to look after. Ramneek, Sophia, Simran and some others belong from this category. These people would often grace the entire class with their occasional presence, and that too on time.

One of my class friends who was there pre-maturely was Kartik. Fuckin 17 years of age and he was with us pursuing graduation. He did not have any beard or moustache back then which made him cute among girls. Poor girls did not know that he was not cute but certainly lacked testosterone. Talking about lack of testosterone, Ravin enters the block! He too was among 'cute' boys in my class. Keeping biological growth aside, Ravin was exceptionally well in dancing, I must say. He was often accompanied by Simran. Simran or Simmu, as I call her resided near Ravin's place. She was open minded and believed in having fun. Studies were secondary to her and the rule for mandatory attendance was the only reason for her to come to the class. She would often bring something tasty for me to eat. While I would enjoy her food, she would take a nap during lectures. I knew how much tired she would be after partying all night. Simran, Meghna and Ramneek were truly devoted to fashion. 'Fashionista' is the term for them. Simran, now-a-days, is doing some studies related to fashion from NIFT. I wish she could be known for her work in future.

Among all Bihari students in my class, Sanket was the one who at least did not look like a labourer. He had maintained good physique and personality. As long as he used to keep his mouth shut, girls would notice and appreciate him. The moment he would open his mouth to utter some shit in a sleepy tone, we all would notice him, with a different intention, though. He wanted to become a model or an actor, I guess. Well… everybody deserves to dream of their dream life. However, he runs his business of filming local weddings. I hope, one day he would film marriages happening outside of Vaishali and Ghaziabad.

I would often go to meet some other friends of mine from different courses inside the bus that JIMS had arranged for them as they would come from far places. I met Priyanka. No, not that Priyanka but the Khaneja one who was in BCA. She was a small packet full of enthusiasm. She held a tremendous flair in her nature. Her one instant look was more than enough for me to feel the euphoria of life. How could I have foreseen what future was bringing to me? We lost contact soon after I was done with my college studies. However, she texts me once a year on friendship day, for sure. I miss her.

In February 2014, I got a chance to intern with NDTV. Since it was my last semester of the degree programme I was supposed to do a field training and submit a report based on that. I had interned with several prominent news channels and newspapers before. Therefore, I was not very enthusiastic about this NDTV one. Little did I know that I was yet to encounter some of the best and worst feelings and experiences that were completely unknown to me.

I was placed with NDTV's Audience Cell, a department which invites and manages everything related to the audience and guests for various talk shows of the channel. That cell was essentially a group of students interning with the channel under the supervision of some other 'recently graduated' students who were working with the channel for who knows how many years! Initially, all I had in my mind was to complete my shift and rush home as it would take almost two hours for me to commute from each side.

Here at NDTV, Khushboo happened. She too was one of the Researchers as I was. We never gave a shit to each other until the day our manager put both of us in a team so as to accomplish an assignment. That was our first close interaction with each other. We both shared our education, background, hobbies, exchanged our numbers and made a hell lot of fun to other colleagues. Who cared about the assignment, anyway? Neither she was going to work there forever nor I was. It was just an internship for us.

From that day onwards, we both used to sit together and exploit company's resources for our personal use. We would spend hours and hours searching for our future colleges and universities and favourite travel destinations. We would show our work published online to each other. Moreover, we used to watch movies in the office. The real fun began when we both would look for another job with some other company while working there at NDTV. It was she who took me to several eating joints which I had only heard of. While we both were living our lives to its fullest, other colleagues were wasting their time calling some random shitty people and requesting them to attend our talk shows.

Amidst all this, I never realised when we became even close friends of each other. I remember, she brought a cake on my 22nd birthday. I had no idea that it was going to happen. That was for the second and last time in my life someone had bothered themselves with my birthday cake. It was Nithya and Simran who did that for the first time in college. That gesture of Khushboo created a special place for her in my mind. I was her fan now. She gave me a chocolate which she knows, I have with me even today. She is pursuing her masters in French. I know she will soon do something crazy!

Khushboo along with my friends at NDTV came for my book launch function at NDWBF 2014 in Pragati Maidan. While others gave me roses, gifts, and bouquets as a token of appreciation, I remember she brought one Minute Maid's pulpy orange for me. I told you we were close friends. I can never thank her enough for being such a sweetheart. All good things come to an end. We never talked to each other on the phone after I left NDTV in April 2014. We seldom text each other now. I wish we could go to TGIF together.

'That would be all I could express here at this point of time about my family, childhood, school, my college and about every moment I have lived with some wonderful people ever created in this world. They all will be with me in my memories, forever and I shall not let those memories die, ever.' I said with a shaky voice. 'I am done, Ma'am,' I told Judy, my IELTS speaking test examiner. I felt a big relief after sharing the experience of my life with her.

'Wow!...Wha...what was that, Gaurav?!' she looked mesmerised. She then nodded her head while making an eye contact with me. 'Well thank you so much for your time. You can check your result online after 13 days of IELTS main exam.' She officially informed me. 'I will check, definitely! Bye now.' I exit the room in a hurry as it was almost two hours since I entered the room for taking the test.

'Where the fuck you have been?' shouted Ranbijay as soon as he saw me coming out of that complex. He looked impatient and hungry.

'Catapulted back in time!' I replied and bought two burgers from a confectionary store.

'How was the test?' asked Ranbijay while hogging that burger.

'It was memorable. Give me my phone back.' I said.

'I think you will score an eight in speaking.' He said.

'We will see, let's go home.'

'What? home? You said we are having dinner together!' he reminded me of my promise.

'Oh! Yes. Let's go to JNU then.' I suggested.

'Perfect.' We both raided JNU.

JNU has many small 'Dhabas' which operate 24 by 7. Food is great and light on the pocket. We both had dinner together. Ranbijay dropped me home and went to his place. After few minutes, I thought of asking him if he reached home or not. I grabbed my phone, what I saw was not unexpected. My phone was loaded with sex applications, nude wallpapers, few pornographic webpages and not to forget, some text messages from Airtel suggesting me to recharge my data balance and talk time. I did not call that dawg and wasted my time cleaning up the mess created by him.

22

REALITY CHECK

I was feeling relaxed that night. Felt as if my mind was free of all worries and thoughts. All I could feel was a glimpse of tranquillity in this disturbed world. I lived a different world in that test room. With all those emotions pumping in my heart, I did not know when I closed my eyes and fell asleep.

It all started when I and Ashwarya were going to college one fine morning in her car. After talking about our previous day, listening to some English and Punjabi songs and sharing what all we did since we last met each other, we stopped at a red signal near Priya's PVR, Vasant Vihar. It usually takes less than a minute to turn that red light into green. But that day was different from other days. There was a huge traffic jam and traffic police were manually coordinating.

'Fuck bhen..cho..!' She shouted in frustration. Drivers in Delhi often go through this kind of hypertension while on the road. I think more than fifty per cent of the stress among all Delhi-ites occur due to traffic jams. I remember Nithya and Krithika giving the same reaction while driving. The only difference is in their swearing. They both never mixed Hindi and English slang together. After swearing a little too much that day, Ashwarya finally shut her mouth. I was smiling at her as she always looked amazing while swearing. She then said she

did not want to live in India anymore and asked me to look upon universities and colleges abroad so that she could pursue her higher studies there, that too along with me. I looked at her surprisingly.

'We will rent an apartment, work part time, cook Maggi and have fun together. Life would be awesome!' She continued. I was wondering for she mentioned everything except studies. Though she had said that due to the frustration she faced on roads of Delhi, yet I took her statement seriously and started researching about some colleges abroad. Her that statement sparked an idea inside my head and I could do anything for that.

My friends in college and my family could see that dedication in me for going abroad. I would spend hours and hours researching on the internet about these countries, their customs, demographics, college rankings and affordability. Ashwarya soon dropped the idea of going out for studies. Probably, she found modelling and living with her boyfriend in Mumbai more comfortable than going abroad with me to study and unlock a whole new world full of opportunities and challenges. Well...talking about comfortability, she literally chose comfort as her option as studying and living abroad without family and friends is not easy at all. However, Ranbijay and Sanket were influenced by my decision and started planning on studying abroad.

I had already completed my graduation from JIMS and taken IELTS academic module. I scored an overall of 7.5 bands out of 9. Judy gave me 7.5 bands out of 9 in speaking test. The next step was to apply in the colleges and universities I had shortlisted. Since I was born in a Punjabi family my choices of countries reflected my genes. I wanted to go to either Canada, Australia, New Zealand, England or Germany to pursue my post-graduate studies. Not only that, I wanted to get settled in one of these countries after I finish my studies.

Therefore, I cut down Germany and England from my list. Typical Punjabi family, I told you. Soon I applied in colleges across these countries. Some colleges demanded academic and professional references. Dr Dhar and Neeru Ma'am were there to help me out. The entire process took three months or so. I got offer letters from all the colleges. Now, I had to make my mind about choosing one of the colleges.

After some serious discussions with my family and friends, researching deeply about selected colleges and countries and some more bullshit, I chose to go to Langara College located in beautiful city of Vancouver, Canada. What was the wait then…I deposited my fee to college, filed my study permit and visa application. VFS Global handles all visa and permit application processing tasks. I got my visa approved on December 5, 2014.

Now it was for sure that I was leaving India for who knows how many years. I got my tickets booked. That was for the first time I had booked a plane ticket ever. I had my first ever flight of my life on December 28, 2014, with Japan Airlines. I was awkwardly excited.

23

Farewell Till We Meet Again

All my college friends, teachers and relatives knew that I had to go to Canada, but fewer knew when was I actually leaving. I did not tell any of my close friends about my departure as I knew they would come to see me off at the airport. I did not want to create a scene there. Actually, I did not want them to make me feel sad or nostalgic.

So, those who did not meet me and did not come to see me off are close to my heart. However, some of my friends who kept me close to their hearts came to see me off. In fact, they came to my house to drop me off to the airport. Shriya, Sahil and Ranbijay came to drop me off. It was really difficult for me to decide whose car I was going to sit in. Relatives arrived few days before my departure. In a blink of an eye, the day arrived when I was all set to fly to Canada via Japan from IGI Airport.

Leema came to my house to say good bye to me. We both saw each other with that egoistic gaze we used to show each other. We both would try not to talk first. Well…this time I had an edge over her. As I was leaving Delhi for a long time, she had to overcome her so called 'ego' and initiate the conversation. I admit, I too was fairly eager to talk to her.

'So, when is your flight?' she asked with a rough voice as if she did not care.

'Midnight.' I replied with even bigger arrogance on my face.

'When am I going to see you again?'

'Well I don't know yet, may be two or three years or so...' I was about to say more but Leema had tears flowing down her cheeks. I was happy to see that love in her eyes. Even before I could say something to pacify her, she hugged me and cried like a baby. I was nervous for a moment as I could not figure out the way to handle that situation. I know how did I keep myself from crying. Though we both used to fight and argue a lot over small issues yet, we were immensely attached to each other. We had grown up together. She always kept me first on her priority list. I miss her very much. Leema left with a smile. She had to go to the office where she was interning.

I started finalising my baggage and took a shower afterwards. Meanwhile, mommy and grandma cooked some food for me. That was the last time I ate home-made food. Indian students have some signature stuff to be taken away with them when they travel abroad. I too had some of the 'Indian' things in my bags. A pressure cooker, Parle-G, Maggi, desi ghee, underwear (a lot of them), some more Maggi, shirts, pants, socks, thermal wear, jackets, *chappals,* soap, some more Parle-G and the list goes on and on. These were some of the things I packed in my bag according to my understanding of life in Canada.

In the evening around five Sahil and Shriya arrived to pick me up for the airport. Minutes later, Ranbijay arrived. Due to conflict between all of us regarding 'where would Gaurav sit?' I asked Ranbijay to leave his car at my home and come with us in Sahil's car. We all finally agreed upon this suggestion. Soon, we all left for the airport. I, Sahil, Shriya and Ranbijay were in one car and rest of my family and relatives were in other four cars. I felt as if I was some influencer kind of person who was being escorted to the airport with five cars in his motorcade.

After thirty minutes of awkward silence in Sahil's car, we reached IGI. Terminal 3 of IGI is amazingly built, I noticed. Everyone was in tears except me. Well…I too was in tears, tears which did not show up in my eyes for I was crying inside my heart. I bid farewell to all my family and friends and entered the facility. There was an officer from CISF who asked for my passport and ticket. I showed him the same and he let me in.

After that moment I could not see my family and friends standing outside the airport. I called and asked them to leave for their destinations. I assured them I would call once I reach Narita International Airport in Tokyo, Japan. They agreed and left. Seconds after, I received Ashwarya's call. She said she was waiting for me outside the airport. I was in absolute stress at that moment. To calm my anger and frustration I swore upon her immensely. I then made her realise the stupidity she did. She never called to inform me that she is coming from Mumbai to meet me in Delhi, and that too in the eleventh hour. She wanted to give me a surprise. Ha Ha…quite a surprise she got for herself! We then talked with each other on phone and bid farewell.

I was very happy and sad at the same time. Happy, for I was finally going to take one of the biggest decisions in my life and sad because I was geographically going very far away from my life, my friends and family. I gathered all my courage and proceeded further inside the airport. While I was standing for my security check after I checked in my baggage, I realised that airports are very easy to navigate. A person can easily get confused or lost at Rajiv Chowk Metro Station but certainly, he/she can never get lost inside an airport given that, they actually want to find their way.

Same is the case with life as well, I discovered. No matter how confused or lost you are in life, if you are willing to find your way you will get back on the right track for sure.

Anyways, I was called by an immigration agent who was supposed to check my passport, boarding pass and visa. I noticed there were few south Indian agents and the remaining majority were Haryanvi. That guy who called me was from Haryana, I could see his accent. He looked at me with a bold face. Needless to say, I gave him a flat expression and he understood he could not boast his authority over me anymore. He then asked for my passport and boarding pass. He scanned and thoroughly checked my visa. And now it was time for some 'stupid questions and smart answers' round.

'Kidh ja riya hai bhai?' (Where are you going, bro?), he asked his first stupid question. He knew I had a Canadian study visa and a ticket to Vancouver. Well…I had to answer him anyhow.

'Sir, Canada!' I replied instantly.

'Hmm…ke karega waha ja ke? (Hmm…what would you do there?), another stupid one.

'Padhai – Post Graduation.' (Study – Post Graduation).

'Kyu…yaha na ho rai tum se padhai?' (Why? Can't you study here?), I was a bit pissed off now.

'Na ji…ab yaha na padhna chah raha main!' (No…I don't want to study here!), I replied with a rough voice in his Haryanvi accent.

The moment I replied him, his face turned pale with distress. I trolled him. You should have seen his face, fucking ugly skunk, I betcha! He stamped my passport and let me pass. The first thing I did after clearing security check was searching for free Wi-Fi at the airport. Luckily, I found one with the grace of GMR Group.

We middle class people are all same from inside. First things first, I logged into my Facebook account and checked-in there as well. You know what, it is more important to check-in on

Facebook than it is to check-in for real at the airport. Let the world which gives zero fucks to what you are doing with your life, know you can afford a plane ticket for economy class. Right?

After sitting at gate number one for half an hour, boarding began. I quickly grabbed my cabin luggage so as to enter in the plane first. It was my first time, I told you. As soon as I thought of running towards the main gate I heard an announcement asking elderly, women with children, first and business class passengers to board respectively. It felt as if someone slapped me right on my face. Then they called premium economy to board. 'One day I will travel in first class.' I made a promise to myself at that very moment. Now, it was us, economy class passengers who were asked to board the plane. Though I had almost complete knowledge of how an aircraft flies, what all happens at airports and what to expect in an emergency, yet I had never experienced it in reality. All thanks to National Geographic's 'Air Crash Investigation' for providing such useful information to me.

I could feel adrenaline rush and butterflies inside my stomach as I proceeded towards the plane. Someone who used to travel in bullock-carts and rickshaws in Bihar and DTC buses in Delhi was going to board an international flight. I saw an airhostess smiling at me and waving. She greeted me and directed me to my seat which was a window one. I clearly remember her smile even now. She was smiling to glory to see me as if we had known each other since ages. Damn! These girls are really good at pretending. I grabbed my seat and started looking outside the window.

Moments after, a Japanese man came and sat next to me. I then remembered I was flying with Japan Airlines. I felt as if I was sitting next to Mr Miyagi of Karate Kid. They all looked same. A few minutes later, my plane began taxiing. The only thing that was bothering me at that moment was the meal they were supposed to serve me. I am a vegetarian since birth, I did not want those Japanese girls to serve something spooky on my plate, rather tray. I had called their office previous day to modify my meal preferences. The lady on the other side could not speak English and I was pretty sure she could not understand me either. The plane speeded up and I could hear the loud noise of its engines. Finally, it took off, probably the best thrilling moment in an aircraft. 'Farewell till we meet again.' I sighed with relief.

24

Welcome to Canada 'Mr. Sharma!'

I never knew when I closed my eyes and fell asleep in my Delhi - Tokyo flight. Since it was all dark outside, I could not see a thing outside my window. However, I witnessed from my window, some cities in India and China glittering with lights. It looked amazing.

Despite the fact, that I could not recognise most of the items in my meal, yet they served me a vegetarian meal, I am sure. After spending about seven hours of watching movies, eating so called fresh food just because it was hot, exploring different areas of the plane and looking what fellow passengers were doing apart from sleeping in that airtight tube, I landed in Tokyo. It was about seven in the morning and raining heavily there. We started getting off from the plane. The same airhostess was standing right next to the door. She looked tired yet she had to smile. I toyed with her idea of being a cabin crew.

I proceeded to a lounge dedicated to serve passengers with connecting flights. Again, I had to check-in on Facebook, which I did. My friends on Facebook whom I barely knew or interacted with were wishing me luck. They were writing motivational statements and other shitty stuff. Well…I acknowledge them for withdrawing two seconds from their 'busy' schedules for me. I then called my family and video-called some of my friends. Narita International had a very good internet connectivity.

After exploring every nook and corner of that airport I was about to board my next flight from Tokyo to Vancouver. The excitement was fairly less this time. I was happy, though, but not anxious. Soon I boarded the flight. Now, Japanese crew was replaced with Canadian ones, passengers were mostly from Canada, China and India, food tasted delicious and I could see outside my window as it was a day for the entire eight-hour journey. Rest all was more or less same as it was in previous flight. I landed at Vancouver International Airport. It was very quiet and peaceful. Airport had fewer people as compared to those at IGI and Narita. I noticed, my Airtel phone was showing Rogers' signal. I had to pass Canada Border Services Agency's check post. I stood in a small line and was called by an officer. Initially, it reminded me of my experience with that Haryanvi immigration officer at IGI. That CBSA officer greeted me with a smile.

'Hi, there! May I please see your passport?' officer requested.

'Sure.' I handed over my passport to him.

'Which college are you enrolled in?' he asked further. This is what smart questioning is all about. That CBSA officer did not ask me what did I come to Canada for, as he had already seen my study visa. Unlike that Haryana guy, this officer knew what to ask and when to ask.

'Langara College, Sir!' I replied happily.

He then scanned my passport and visa quickly. 'You are now good to go! Welcome to Canada Mr. Sharma!' he said and let me pass. I was in absolute relief now. I had finally entered Canada and became 'Mr. Sharma' from Gaurav and Shanu.

I collected my baggage and rushed outside the airport. Automatic gates opened and I felt a strong chilly wave of wind. I instantly entered back inside the gate. 'I am in Canada.' I thought indeed. I had a word with Manjeet Uncle, our family friend who was living in Vancouver those days. He had assured me to provide initial accommodation until I find a better apartment or suite to live in. I called him and he said he will be there to pick me up in fifteen minutes or so.

Meanwhile, I thought of calling home. I video-called home and informed everyone about my safe arrival to Canada. Grandma asked me to confirm if I had landed in Canada and not any other country. I just pointed my camera towards the different direction where grandma could see some Sardar roaming here and there. *'Aa ta Kanedda hi lagda hai.'* (it is Canada, indeed) grandma said in joy. We all laughed like anything.

Before Manjeet uncle could come to pick me up, I was able to post my final check-in on Facebook. I also managed to update my location on all other social platforms such as Twitter and LinkedIn. Soon uncle arrived with his son and my friend Micky. We met each other and proceeded to the City of Burnaby which shares its border with Vancouver.

We reached Maple Place Towers which was a beautiful apartment building. Micky had some of his friends from college living in that apartment. We reached the eleventh floor via lift. I met three guys who were living in that apartment where I was supposed to spend some days until I arrange for an accommodation for myself. Uncle and Micky soon left.

Everything was going well until I got to know that those three guys were from Pakistan. I had always heard about Pakistan and to be honest, most of the times what I had heard about Pakistan or read about it was not good at all. News related to terrorism, crime, unemployment, poverty and what not.

Moreover, I had a preconceived notion that most of the Pakistanis are extremists. Also, that most of them are dumb as fuck which is correct, though. Eventually, after living with those guys I realised that not all who belong from Pakistan are bad, dumb or extremists. Those three guys, Harris, Ammar and Nitesh were almost same as I was. They too had come to Canada to pursue their higher studies. They too had a common sense which makes them unique as we all are. Above all, they were very helpful and cooperative. They were like me; they were human beings like all of us are. They had a big TV, fast internet and Play Station 3. All four of us really got along with each other.

One week had passed and I asked Ammar and Harris to take me to the nearest grocery store where I could find some vegetarian Indian food. They took me to Real Canadian Superstore A.K.A. Superstore. It was like Big Bazars we have in India but lot bigger than that. I soon raided its aisle mentioned 'International Food Section'. What I saw was more than enough to restore my faith in God again. I saw Frooti, Maggi, Parle-G, MDH Masala, Chips, Ketchup and everything else I would see in a grocery store in India.

That day brought a new hope in my heart. It was confirmed that food would not be a problem for me in Canada. Now I was all set to go to my college next day.

25

A College Where India and China Co-exist, Peacefully!

At first sight, Langara seems not just a college but a multicultural sub-city in itself. A dominion where students from all across the world come to earn higher learning. More than twenty thousand students graduate from Langara College annually, greater than students graduating annually from most of the colleges in Delhi.

However, when I started my college I noticed that most of the students were either from China or India. To be more specific, from China and Punjab. After my orientation session on January 5, 2015, I started getting used to the building structure. I also got to see some of my classmates who were going to be with me for next four semesters.

I remember the first day of my college. It was statistics' class supposed to be taken by Mr Michael Lo. I reached before time as always. Soon a Chinese guy who looked like Jakie Chan entered with a tab in his hand. I thought he was a student, but turned out he was Michael. He smiled at me and in return I smiled at him. He then got busy with his arrangements for projectors and computers. Minutes later, a Sardar came in class.

I was not surprised as I was expecting some Punjabi people in my class. I was in Canada, I reminded myself.

After some more time, a group of students came which had three or four more Sardars, some Punjabi girls and some other boys from Punjab. 'What the…hell!' I thought. My class was full of Punjabi people AKA 'The Desi.' Before I could lose my hope entirely in Canadian education system, I saw three girls entering my class. They were certainly not from India. I got some boost from inside my heart. After that, I saw some more students coming to my class who were not from India. Now I was relieved.

My college life in Langara was not as engaging as that was in JIMS. I had to study full time, work part-time, cook food or to make arrangements for that, shop for groceries, clean my house, do my laundry and above all, I was all by myself here in Canada. I remember my teachers in Langara, they too were from different countries. Canada is the land of immigrants.

One big difference in colleges of North America is the way teachers teach. Here, they are not teachers but instructors, for they do not teach you, they instruct you. You are allowed to come anytime in the class, you don't have to say 'may I come in?', you can use your mobile phones and laptops and do whatever you want to do without disturbing rest of the class, you can eat your food or drink coffee and above all, you can wear anything you want. Nobody gives a shit to what you do. In sophisticated words, nobody cares! I myself attended my college wearing *chappals* and pyjamas. Interactions are formal, devoid of any intimate connection, people are busy in their phones and laptops and despite being connected every moment, they are miles apart from each other.

One thing that I liked very much in Canada was the decency in people to respect each other's freedom. Nobody would judge you here if you kiss your girlfriend or boyfriend in public. You can do whatever you want without disturbing the peace and integrity of the community which you live in.

I remember my instructor Ron. He was very good at what he taught, Negotiation Skills. The only thing you want to keep in mind if you want to attend his classes was to enter the class before he does. He would shut and lock the door immediately after entering the class.

Another instructor was Vicky. She was my accounts teacher and probably the sweetest personality in Langara College. Her subject i.e., financial and managerial accounting was very boring but somehow her classes turned out to be very interesting.

One instructor who always motivated me was Natasha. She was my CO-OP instructor. In Canada, career placement department of a college or university is called CO-OP department. Natasha was from Serbia but knew many languages such as Serbian, English, Greek and Czech. Impressive! Isn't it? She was meditative by temperament and I don't know how could she keep herself under control all the time. One could really learn how to simplify things in life from her.

Through ups and downs of my academic life in Langara, I made my way out. I graduated from my college on June 8th, 2016. I was happy for it was my first convocation ceremony of life as I could not attend my bachelor's convocation in JIMS; I was in Vancouver then. Also, I had a Canadian education at post graduate level which was going to help me shape my future in Canada.

26

My 'Canadian' Friends

During my first year spent in Vancouver, I met some unique people, made few good friends in college and outside college and developed a sense of belongingness for the community where I lived.

I came across Amanpreet, my classmate in Langara and a Delhi-ite. I remember when I first saw him in class, he was taking pride in asking each and every instructor about passing marks in their respective subjects. Seemed like he already knew what was bothering rest of the students regarding studies, as we all wanted to know how high was the passing mark. I was pondering upon his confidence and openness in class. Little did I know that he was going to be my best friend in Canada. I was in need of an accommodation and hence I started asking my classmates if they needed one as well. I and Amanpreet talked to each other and soon realised we both wanted to rent one independent accommodation. He was living at his relative's place in Burnaby. I also confirmed with him if he is vegetarian or not. I could not live with anyone who eats non-veg food. He said he used to eat meat before, but since past eight years he had not. By the way, I am highly indebted to the elderly couple, Anita Nani and Kuldeep Nana Ji for they had always treated me equally as they would treat Amanpreet.

Next day, after attending college we both started searching for a rental apartment or basement or whatever suited us. After two hours of extensive search on Fraser Street, we finally found a basement which was appealing. We agreed to rent that basement of Mr Bhullar, a Desi.

We both were happy as things seemed to fall in right spots. We would go to college and come to home together. We found jobs at the same gas station (petrol pump) which was Husky Energy, Canada's very own integrated energy company. Life was going well. I was managing my living expenses in Vancouver without asking my family to send me money. They had paid for my college fee and therefore all of their savings were drained.

I also met Bhuvan and Preetpal in my class. Bhuvan was from Delhi whereas, Preetpal had spent his childhood in Uttar Pradesh and adulthood in Punjab. Bhuvan was more sophisticated and mature as he was 28 then and had a girlfriend who, as Bhuvan claimed, was with him with past nine years while on the other hand, Preetpal was 22 and full of life. All he wanted was good food, good money and sexy girls around him.

I soon got to know Amanpreet was two years elder than me. I discovered he was a firm believer in God and always tried to give back to the society according to his capacity. The degree of devotion to God he held was at par with the degree of my denial to 'his' existence. Now, an atheist and a believer would often engage in arguments. We had many healthy debates and some harsh conversations as well. No matter what happened, we always had our dinner together. I wish either he or I or we both could win Lotto Max and/or 6-49 so as to get each other's life well settled.

Another friend of mine in Vancouver was Anmolpreet. Initially, I did not even speak to any of the girls in my college.

As time passed by, my classmates got to know about me and vice-versa. Though there was no girl in our class from Delhi, yet some of the girls had an open minded thought process which made them different from traditional and typical Punjabi girls who are more conservative and sophisticated in nature. Anmolpreet seemed to be a decent girl to me from the very beginning. She would often keep in touch with me. She would interact on a regular basis and share her views and opinions with me to constitute a common conscience. Even now when we are not in college anymore, she texts me frequently to ask about how my life is going on. Moreover, Anmolpreet trusted me unconditionally. I don't know if she trusts everybody so easily and equally as she trusts me. I am ever grateful to her for being such a good friend.

Whenever I talk about trust, I remember Aarsh, my classmate and dear friend from Langara. I was never being able to figure out if she was naïve or clever. However, one thing was for sure, that she trusted me blindly. She would not mind sharing her personal life with me. Moreover, she would easily provide me with her confidential information as required by me to assist her in doing official banking and immigration formalities. There were times when I had to remind her about her openness and carelessness. She would never take me seriously. Aarsh was short tempered and happy go lucky at the same time. Like me, she could never keep things in her mind and always spoke about it freely. She was empathising in nature. However, she often used to talk to me whenever she needed my help or advice. This nature of her makes her mean up to some extent, I would comment. Whatever her nature be in life, I wish her success and luck and would ask her to keep in touch with friends even if she does not need them.

My friend Loveleen went to Douglas college in New Westminster after completing one semester at Langara. I don't know the exact reason behind her that decision. Some said she had a boyfriend in Douglas while others claimed she had one in Langara who broke up with her. I don't know what was the truth but one thing was for sure, that she was my buddy in Langara. The only girl whom I was friends with since the first day of the college. She reminds me of Dhun sometimes as both of them left my college and went to some other one. Loveleen and I barely talk now but I am sure we would never be able to forget our days in Langara.

Whether it is Delhi, Punjab or Vancouver one thing is for sure that clashes and disputes are inevitable where Desi people meet. I witnessed some of the conflicts in Langara as well. While fights and arguments in JIMS used to be more violent and included the use of physical touch, here in Langara people had verbal fights only. It is really a big issue here if you touch any other person.

I remember, in JIMS, Ranbijay had a fight with Vanshaj AKA 'Jazz Man', as my classmates would call him I don't know why. It was more of a planned fight than an accidental clash, I got to know later. I guess it was our fifth semester's end term exam scheduled at Trinity Institute in Dwarka. I was eating pasta with Ashwarya in her car. Suddenly, I heard a different thwack which was loud. I soon realised what was about to happen there. Seeing Ranbijay and Vanshaj together was like keeping fuel and fire together. You never know when it would catch fire. I and some other classmates rushed towards both of them. By the time we reached there and separated them, Ranbijay had punched Vanshaj so much so that his nose became blood red. I am sure Jazz Man had also boxed or slapped Bihari Babu several times. That fight gave a chance to all other boys in my class to spit out their frustration on Vanshaj. I remember Rohit, Sagar, Sanket and few other guys also tried to punch Vanshaj. Well, I am not sure if all of them were to harm him or not, yet it seemed that way. I was thinking about Amanpreet (Jazz Man's girlfriend). How would she had felt at that very moment?

Meghna must have done some good deeds in her past as she was never with Vanshaj. I had presumed she would be his girlfriend soon, as Jazz Man had a serious inclination towards Meghna. I had seen that video in which he was chanting Maghna's name and Sagar was ranting Parijat's. That fight was one of the most stupid acts performed by two formally educated yet uncultured beings of modern times.

Anyways, leaving Delhi aside, I had seen some conflicts between my friends in Langara as well. I remember when Preetpal and Aarsh had a desi argument fight backed up with some swearing in Ron's class. Preetpal also had a cold war like situation with Karambir, Prasad and Aarsh developed some disturbances in their friendship and so many other quarrels took place.

There were some hidden love stories cooking in my class. They were more of one sided love. I remember, Preetpal had a crush on Parampreet, Bhuvan too would show his interest in Parampreet in a casual manner. Some guys in my class really liked Aarsh. Supreet and Jaspreet were other girls who were being secretly admired by some of my friends. I would not name that guy who had a secret crush on Loveleen. Preetpal essentially was ever ready to make bonds with girls in my college. He had this socialising skill in them since their childhood. Amidst all this, I was still figuring out the way to cook roti, rice and sabzi for myself.

One person who was, in some way or the other, an integral part of my life spent in Vancouver was Balpreet. Ballu, as I would call her with fondness, was customer service representative i.e., teller in Scotiabank. As I had my Canadian bank account maintained with Scotiabank, I would always visit that branch so as to get my cheques deposited, withdraw cash or to do some other formalities. Initially, I would simply go to the branch and get my work done with the help of anyone available to assist customers until I met Ballu for a couple of times. After we had some interactions with each other, I felt it convenient and comfortable to talk with Ballu. Now, everybody in the bank knew that I would always go to Ballu's desk. She was aware of this habit of mine.

She too was a Punjabi; a 'Desi Sweet' dipped in 'Canadian *Chashni*'. Her spoken Punjabi wrapped with Canadian accent would make me go sweet on her, inside my mind. We would always share instances from our lives with each other. Moreover, Ballu always understood my situation as an international student in Canada. She would often empathise and provide me with useful information that helped me a lot in sustaining. I wish, I could show Ballu the respect and appreciation I had for her in my heart. Now that I have moved from Vancouver to Victoria, the capital city of British Columbia, banking with Scotiabank is no fun. She is being missed badly. I wish her all the very best for her future endeavours.

27

DELHI CALLING

After I was done with my studies in Vancouver, I planned to visit my family and friends in Delhi. History was about to repeat itself.

It was in the month of March when I and Amanpreet got our tickets booked for Delhi. We had our flights with KLM on May 3rd, 2016 from Vancouver to Delhi via Amsterdam. Soon the day arrived and we both left for Delhi. I was excited and thoughtful about my trip as I was going to notice some differences between lifestyles of Vancouver and Delhi. I landed at IGI. It reminded me of my days when I was planning to go to Canada. I soon collected my baggage and came out.

Brother, papa, and chachu were there to receive me. I did not tell any of my friends about my trip to India. The moment I came out of the airport, I felt a hot wave of the wind on my face. I reminded myself that I was in Delhi. While crossing the road I was looking for zebra crossing which I could not find there. I became nervous about crossing the road. Since past one year and a half, I had never jaywalked on the road. But I had to, in Delhi. Another problem was traffic on roads, honking and dusty air. I realised Vancouver was much better place to live. The only reason that makes Delhi superior from Vancouver apart from my family and friends being in Delhi is food. Delhi's food is incredible. I did not realise that until I left Delhi.

I had booked my IELTS General Training module in Delhi. I had to take that module so as to get my permanent residency filed in Canada. I missed Ashley Judy while taking speaking test. This time, some fat aunty was there to take my test. She asked me to speak about the first bicycle I got. How the fuck I could remember my first cycle. Even if I do, what do I speak about it? That it has two tyres, one handle and paddles! Is this what helps them in measuring my spoken English proficiency? I was disturbed but I had to take the test anyway.

After few days, I also went to my college, JIMS to collect my bachelor's degree as I missed my convocation for being in Vancouver. I went along with Kartik, that testosterone lacking chap. Seeing my college after a long time reminded me of my college days. Almost everything seemed same as it was two years before. However, many of my teachers left the college and joined somewhere else. Probably, chairman of my college was paying less to my teachers than what they deserved. He could do this as he was a *baniya,* I had heard several times before, from my friends in college. They were stupid I told you.

Time in Delhi passed quicker than ever. I did not realise when one month was over and I had my return flight to Vancouver. One day before my departure, I met Sahil and Shriya. I could not keep myself from meeting them. They are my *'Janakpuriya Chhap'* friends after all. We had dinner in District Centre together. Next day, I met Roopa in the morning. Leema and her family were already in the USA as they got their Green Cards after eight years of applying. At around ten in the night, I booked an Ola cab for the airport. Ola and Uber are doing really good business in Delhi. My return flight was with KLM as well. After 17 hours of tiring journey, I reached Vancouver. I noticed there was no excitement or anxiety left in me. Flying became boring. After reaching Vancouver, I had to figure out what I was going to do with my life. Since studies were over and

I had been given three years of work permit by Citizenship and Immigration Canada, I had to look for a job that would help me in filing my PR in Canada.

I consulted some of my known in Vancouver and it was decided that moving to Victoria would be beneficial as far as job hunting is concerned.

28

I Am a Victorian!

I soon moved to Victoria, the capital city of British Columbia. It takes approximately two hours from Vancouver to Victoria in ship (ferry, as we call it here). Preetpal and Amanpreet also moved with me initially. Soon Preetpal left for Vancouver, he did not like it here in Victoria as it is very hard to find Desi people. Preetpal had lived in UP and Punjab and was fond of Desi people.

Victoria is a very beautiful city. Though it was very difficult to make a permanent move to Victoria, yet we were hopeful for new opportunities and better future. It was hard for me to leave everything at once as I knew I was not going to see Vancouver, my friends from college, Ballu and my known for a long time. I found one beautiful apartment located in the lap of nature in Victoria. I soon got settled in that new city. Things were seeming to be good to us.

However, there were times when I would feel lonely and helpless in Victoria. Visiting my family in recent past, leaving Vancouver for a long term, hunting for a decent job and finding it hard to settle down in Victoria initially, were some of the reasons behind me not being at my peace.

It was then when Himani happened. I had contacted her few days before I had to move to Victoria. She was working with a publisher in Delhi. Since I was about to complete my novel I wanted to do some research about publishers in advance. It would have saved my time and fastened publication process. Hence, I asked Himani if her publisher could publish an autobiographical fiction or not. Himani was my junior in JIMS. I would often see her roaming here and there in college with her friends. Though we both had an idea about each other in college yet, we never really talked or interacted as such. We just knew about each other of being in same college and department.

Anyways, I texted her on Facebook about my concern. After an hour or so, I noticed she had seen my text but did not reply back. I was little disappointed then. Actually, I did not really expect an ignoring notion from her side. Since we never had a word with each other in college, we had a formal rapport built between us. Needless to say, it was she who sent me request to connect on Facebook and LinkedIn. In fact, there are very few people who had this privilege of me wanting them to connect on social platforms. I had an ego problem, I told you. Moreover, I never really felt the need of socialising or interacting with others.

One day had passed and I did not hear from her. Now, it was too much for me to handle. I thought she did not want to cater to my concern and therefore, it was not right to bug her off again regarding that. 'What is the point of being in her friend's list if I create problems for her? There is no point of being connected on social media when you are not willing to socialise.' I thought...probably, I overthought.

And I unfriended Himani from my Facebook immediately with a heavy heart. I soon got busy with my wrapping and packing as I was preparing to leave Vancouver. Suddenly, I heard a beep and saw that it was Himani replying me on Facebook messenger. She then told me that her taking confirmation from the director of publishing company about my concern took one day to reply me. She wanted to provide me with authentic information. I appreciated her efforts and confessed about me unfriending her from FB. I apologised and instantly sent her a request which she accepted. Himani handled the situation wisely. In a way, she was now among those few privileged to accept my request on FB. Haha!

That day our conversation on FB went for two more hours. She asked me about my studies in Canada, the progress of my debut novel, she shared her future plans of studying further and going abroad. To the best of my knowledge and belief, I answered her each and every question.

We both then realised that it had been a very long time since we both had that long conversation with anybody. While I had started counting my calories intake and calories burned every day, Himani remained thoughtful about what she would have for lunch and dinner. Also, I discovered that she takes time to open up but once she feels comfortable talking to you, she talks too much! Luckily, she talks sense. I came to know that we both had many similarities in our nature. One big difference was she believing in God and I being religiously an Atheist.

Despite our contrasting characters, we developed a stronger bond between us. Eventually, we exchanged our numbers and started talking to each other almost on a daily basis. Now that it's a new experience for me as well, I have no idea where this will take me in future. For now, I just wish she could attain whatever she wants in her life. And you, yes you there…bear with me and keep in touch!

29

The Crux

That was all I could express here about my life and people associated with me. Those who know me well do not need a book to know about me. For those who did not know me before, I would like to convey my gratitude to you for investing your valuable time in something created by a (so far) nobody. Big thanks for picking up an unknown name despite hundreds of thousands of famous authors being there in the market.

Well, this is how things are in present times…

I lately got approached by my college friend Neha. She was my junior in JIMS. She had some work related queries. Also, she had used my textbooks to gain supplementary knowledge about respective subjects. However, she did not really need my books to study as she is at par with me as far as academic concepts are concerned. What makes her out of the league is her secretive nature. Despite being in touch with her I have never heard her voice or seen her so far. I hope her ultra-reserved nature does not malign her decency and integrity among her friends. She, by the way asks so many questions, which shall make her an active learner. I remember when, her being clandestine created a panic inside my mind. I was worried if I was sharing my knowledge with and investing my time in the right person or not. I had then asked Neeru Ma'am about her. After knowing that she exists actually, I was relieved. After few days, we had a conversation via skype audio; two days after, on skype video. How could I have foreseen, that video call was going to be the very first and last time I would see her. Despite being very simple and beautiful, Neha remained conscious about her looks. My present apartment number in Victoria is exactly same as that of Neha's apartment, sheer coincidence! We were in touch for less than a month, yet we knew almost everything going in each other's life. My best wishes to her.

I am in Victoria with Amanpreet. Preetpal is in Vancouver. We three think that Bhuvan is married to his girlfriend and might have a child. He is working in a Subway restaurant by the way.

Anmolpreet entered corporate world and is working in Surrey. She is a book worm.

Prashant is living his so called student life in Texas, US. I am worried he is becoming bald.

Shubhendu and Vivek are sailing the sea with pride. They talk to me whenever they hit the shore.

Ranbijay and Sanket are presently living together in Melbourne, Australia. Apart from having sex with different foreign girls on a regular basis, they sometimes study as well. It would not be their fault if they ever begin to objectify girls in near future as they had been treated by their respective girlfriends in such a manner in their past. It's true, that not all men are dogs, some women are bitches indeed.

Priya, Swati and all other friends in that cool group of my class are busy making their lives better. Some opened their own business, some joined their family business.

Some are studying further in the hope of getting a decent job while some are working to save some money for their further studies!

Ashwarya is still in Mumbai doing photo shoots. I don't know if she has quit smoking or not. She has got approval from her parents about her boyfriend, whom she would be (apparently) married with. But that still does not allow me to share what was happened that day between me and her!

Dhun still lives nearby my home in Delhi. She might still be going to Sonu Juice Corner. One hell of a girl she was!

Krithika is damn sure she will be an IAS officer one day. She has to...okay leave it. I am damn sure if she is damn sure she can do anything and every damn thing, for sure!

Nithya has done her Masters and probably working hard...or hardly working, who knows. Someone get me some Idli Sambhar, please!

Shriya is trying to get a new job that could be of her interest.

Sahil, on the other hand, is assisting his dad in their business. His website/blog justgosahil.com is doing well.

The trio of fashionistas in my college, i.e., Simran, Meghna and Ramneek are busy and doing well in their lives. However, they somehow withdraw some time for posting their 'pouting' pictures on Facebook. I told you they are truly devoted to fashion.

Apart from posting her pictures with copied captions on Facebook, Shraddha works with Telenor in Lucknow. She is showing great courage at work as doing field jobs in India are not easy at all. I don't think she is that sophisticated anymore, as she used to be in school. We started talking to each other few days ago. Then I picked up a fight with her over nothing as such. Since then we never really talked. I hope things will be alright. I told you I am weird.

Leema was in the US lately, with her family. They all are working hard to make their livelihoods better. I shall visit her family soon. She was planning to take admission in Jamia Millia Islamia under NRI quota. She has a boyfriend (which is fourth or fifth one I guess) in Delhi as well. Probably, that is why she developed an urge to study further in Delhi, despite being in the USA. Anyways, she went back to Delhi in August 2016 to pursue her masters from JMI in the field of Human Resource Management. Someone who always needs my advice and approvals before doing anything important in life, now wishes to manage human resource for a company. Irony died a million times, right here!

Khushboo lives in Pondicherry. She is doing her masters in French. She is crazy AF. Dude, you better go to that expensive bakery college in France which has a name I still can't pronounce correctly. Vogue often has openings for its New York office, by the way!

Himani keeps herself so damn busy in her work and studies that she can give a tough challenge even to the POTUS. Her dreams are bigger and stronger than clutches of incapability in life. She shall achieve them all.

Dhar Sir got his debut novel 'Orphans of the Storm' published and working on his second novel. Rest of what he shared with me about his life shall remain in my mind.

And here I am in Victoria, searching out for the best fitness application to work with Fitbit Surge, Jaybird X2 and iPhone 6s combined. I wake up every day with a panic inside my mind about what to make for my breakfast and lunch. Being unable to execute my skills in the kitchen, I often survive on Vega Sports

Performance Protein Shake. And of course! Maggi, Bread and butter are always there for me!

I peep into my phone several times a day to see bus schedules, bank balance, credit card statements, bills, GPS, click pictures and for knowing the time. Calling and chatting with friends and family has become a matter of past decade.

Frequent power cuts, pollution, population, Delhi Metro, crowded DTC buses, lots of Haryanvi people, mosquitoes, friends and family, foes, slow internet connections, awesome street food, homemade food, fuckin hot summers, traffic jams, chicks with overflowing attitude just because they know how to speak intermediate English, boys with third class motorbikes, animals on roads, love birds at bus stops, Radio Mirchi, RaGa, NaMo and Arvind Kejriwal...all are missing here in Canada. However, we in Canada have many people full of shit, just like we have in India or anywhere in the world. This one pooping similarity between Canada and India often restores my faith in 'Vasudhaiv Kutumbakam' (The world is one family) thing!

Gaurav is a man, man is a social being and Gaurav is not social at all. From statements one two and three we get 'Gaurav is just a being.' Hence proved, he mere exists.

I don't know where I am, what am I doing, where will life take me, how will things go, whom to talk to, what to share, what to cook, how to eat, when to sleep, what to wear, what to do and how to live. All of my known are busy making their CVs look professional and substantial. And I am figuring out the way to make my life normal and less bumpy. Forget about building strong resume. Rest assured, I am okay...I will be alright. Cheers to my life!

* * * *